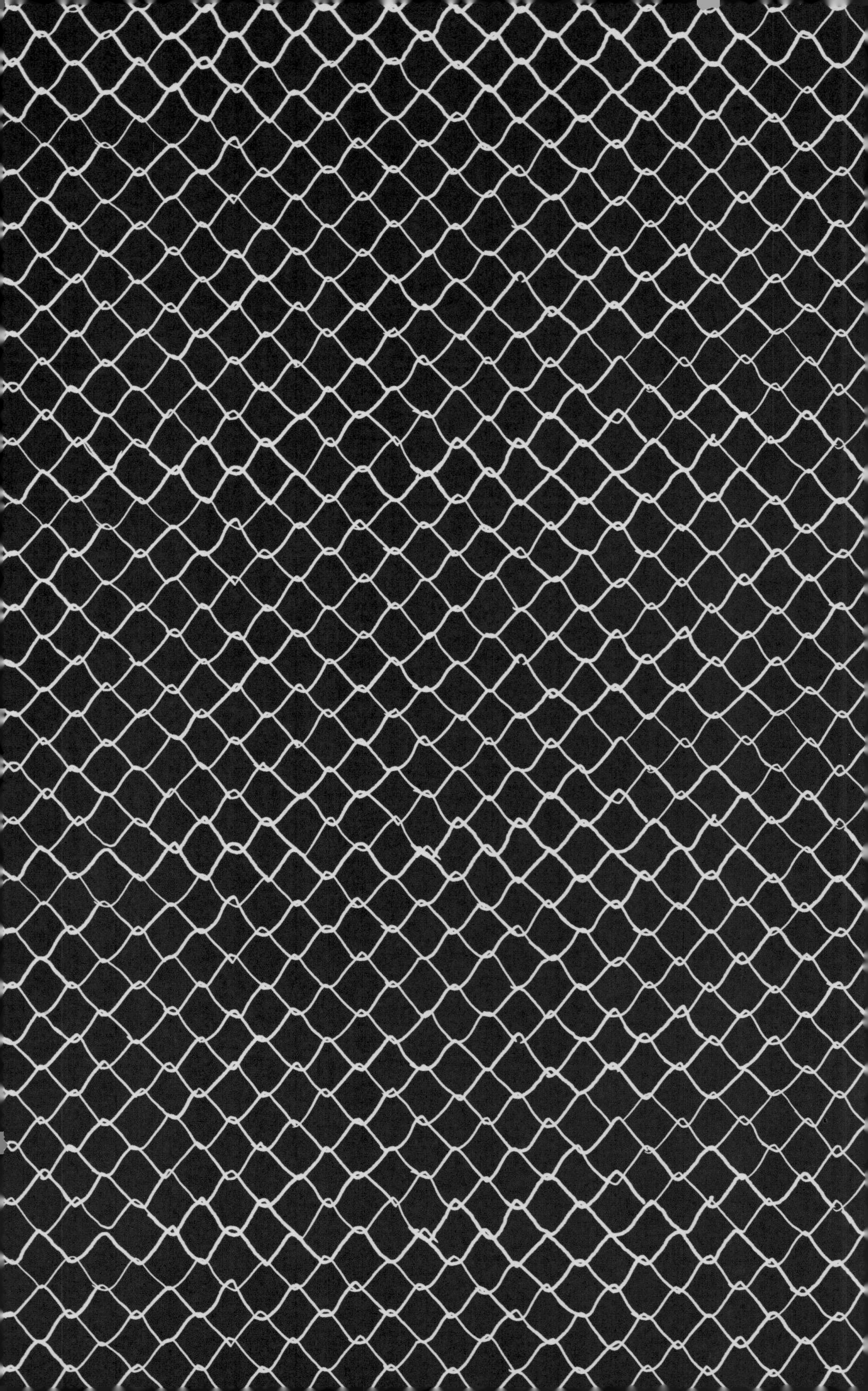

No!

No sun – no moon!
   No morn – no noon –
No dawn –
   No sky – no earthly view –
   No distance looking blue –
No road – no street – no "t'other side the way "–
   No end to any Row –
   No indications where the Crescents go –
   No top to any steeple –
No recognitions of familiar people –
   No courtesies for showing 'em –
   No knowing 'em!
No traveling at all – no locomotion,
No inkling of the way – no notion –
   "No go" – by land or ocean –
   No mail – no post –
   No news from any foreign coast –
No park – no ring – no afternoon gentility –
   No company – no nobility –
No warmth, no cheerfulness, no healthful ease,
   No comfortable feel in any member –
No shade, no shine, no butterflies, no bees,
No fruits, no flowers, no leaves, no birds,
   November!

Thomas Hood (1844)

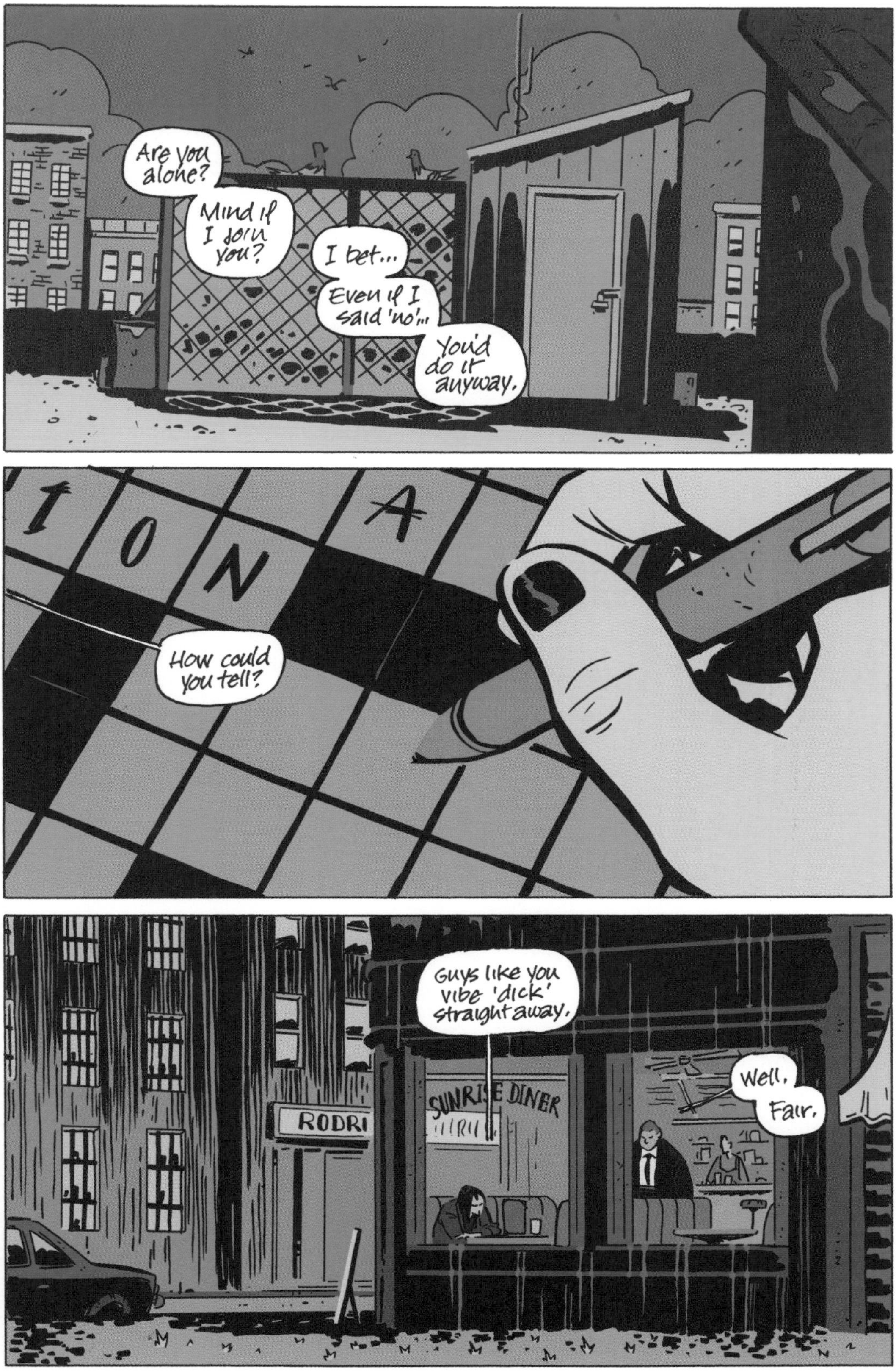
Are you alone?
Mind if I join you?
I bet...
Even if I said 'no'...
You'd do it anyway.
TION
A
How could you tell?
SUNRISE DINER
RODRI
Guys like you vibe 'dick' straight away.
Well.
Fair.

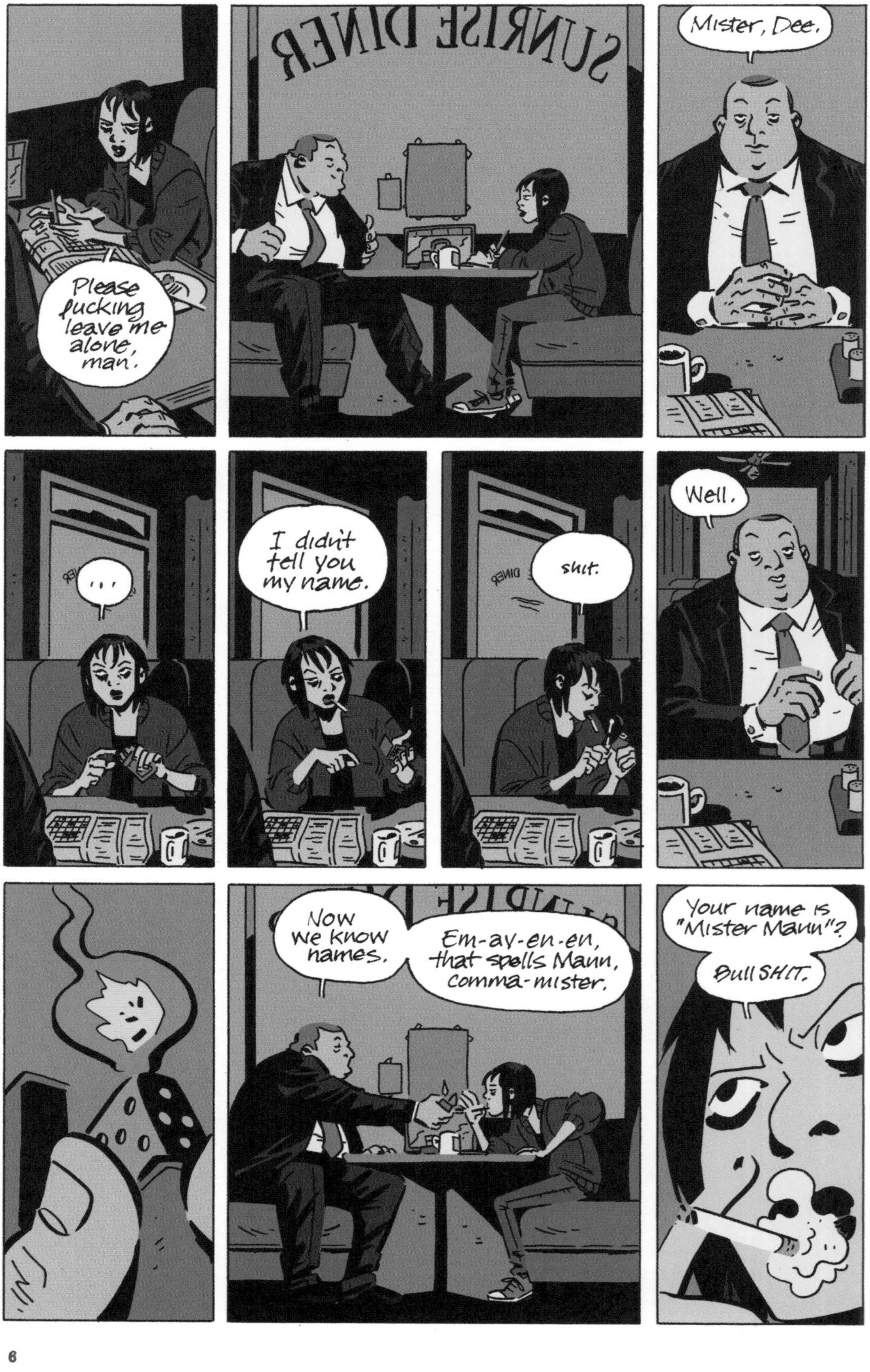
Please fucking leave me alone, man.
SUNRISE DINER
Mister, Dee.
...
I didn't tell you my name.
shit.
Well.
Now we know names.
Em-ay-en-en, that spells Mann, comma-mister.
Your name is "Mister Mann"?
BullSHIT.

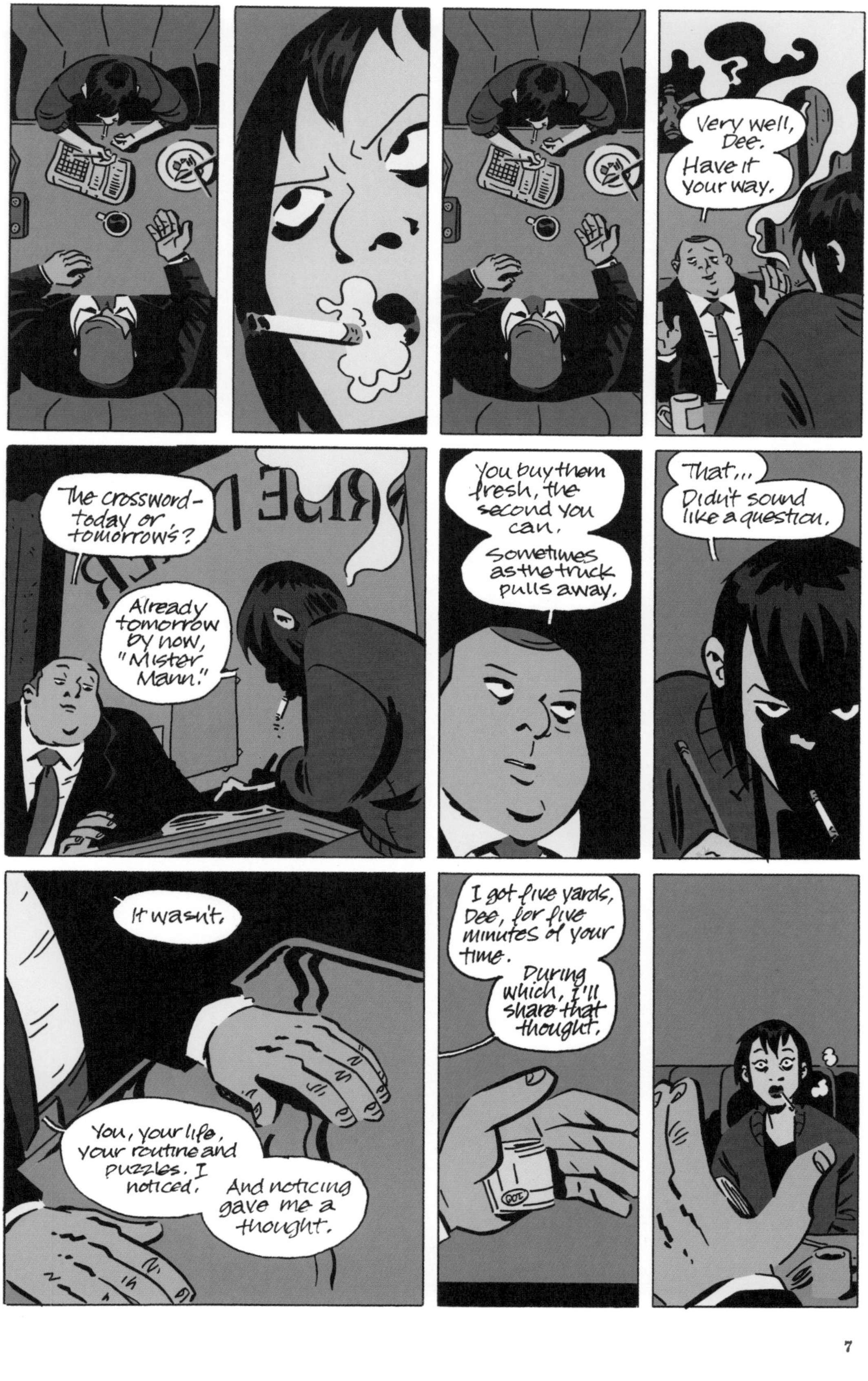

Very well, Dee. Have it your way.
The crossword - today or tomorrow's?
Already tomorrow by now, "Mister Mann."
You buy them fresh, the second you can.
Sometimes as the truck pulls away.
That,,, Didn't sound like a question.
It wasn't.
You, your life, your routine and puzzles. I noticed.
And noticing gave me a thought.
I got five yards, Dee, for five minutes of your time.
During which, I'll share that thought.

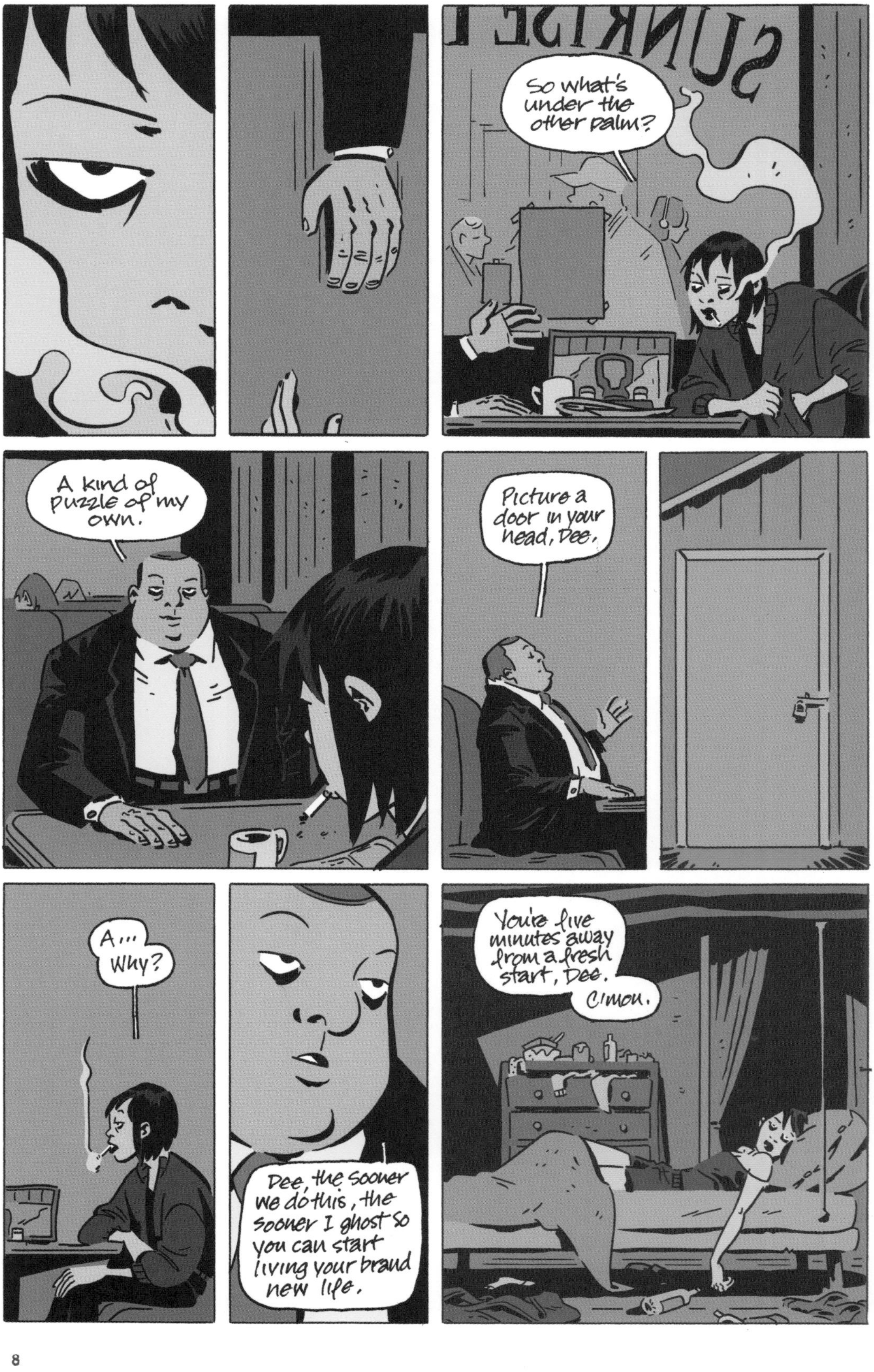
SUNRISE
So what's under the other palm?
A kind of puzzle of my own.
Picture a door in your head, Dee.
A... Why?
Dee, the sooner we do this, the sooner I ghost so you can start living your brand new life.
You're five minutes away from a fresh start, Dee.
C'mon.

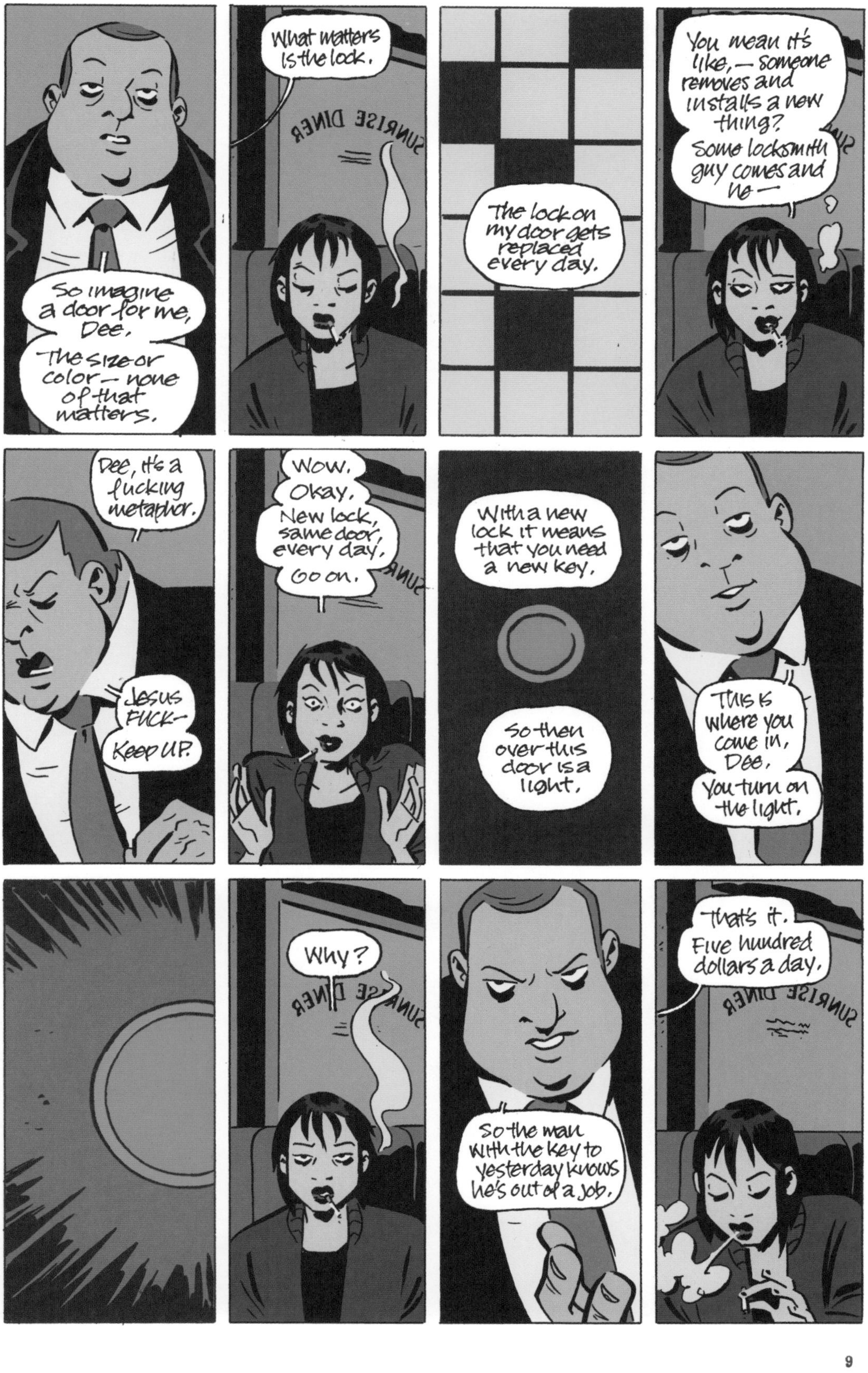

So imagine a door for me, Dee.
The size or color— none of that matters.
What matters is the lock.
SUNRISE DINER
The lock on my door gets replaced every day.
You mean it's like,— someone removes and installs a new thing?
Some locksmith guy comes and he—
Dee, it's a fucking metaphor.
Jesus FUCK-
Keep UP.
Wow.
Okay.
New lock, same door, every day.
Go on.
With a new lock it means that you need a new key.
So then over this door is a light.
This is where you come in, Dee.
You turn on the light.
Why?
SUNRISE DINER
So the man with the key to yesterday knows he's out of a job.
That's it.
Five hundred dollars a day.
SUNRISE DINER

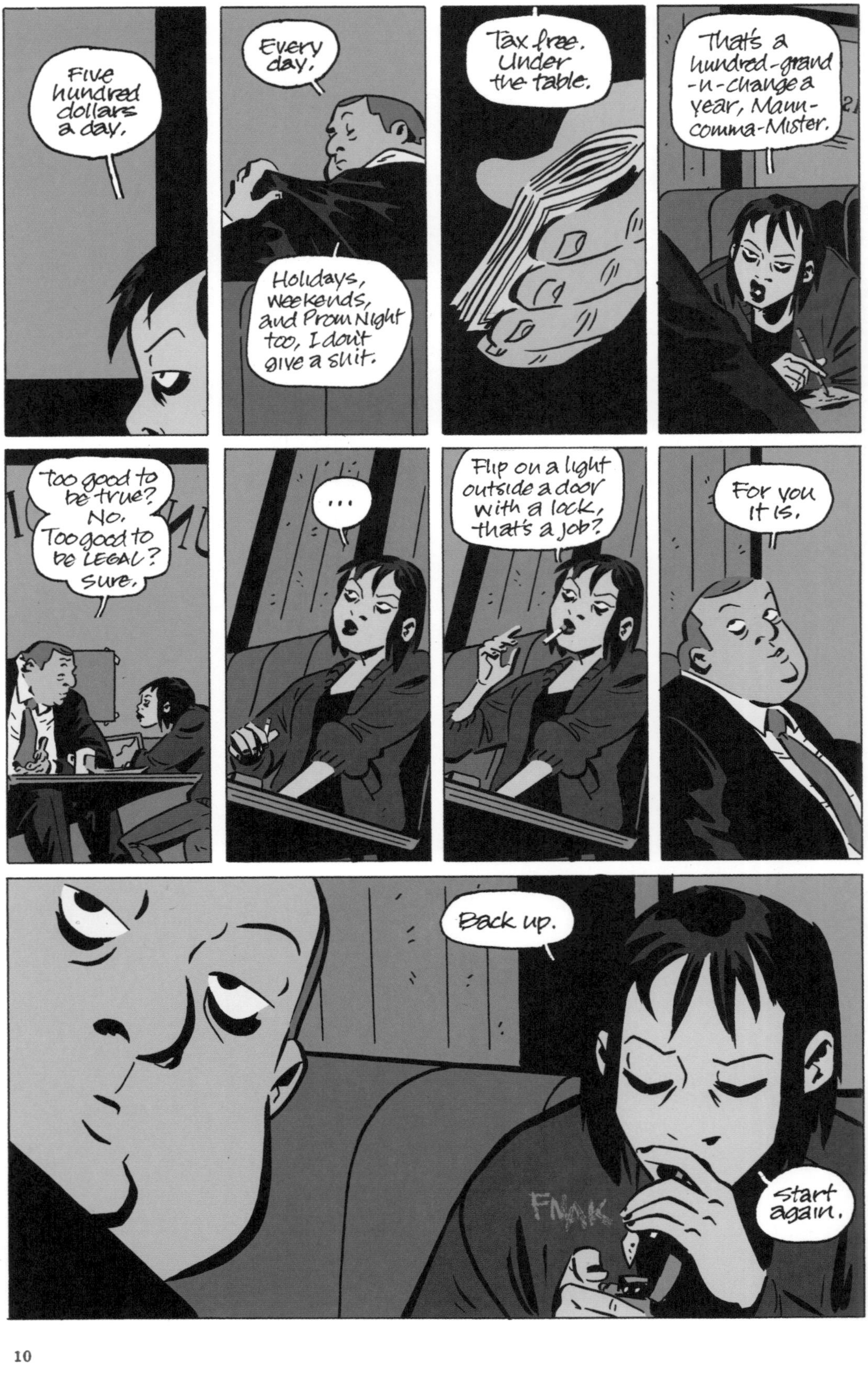
Five hundred dollars a day.
Every day.
Holidays, weekends, and Prom Night too, I don't give a shit.
Tax free. Under the table.
That's a hundred-grand-n-change a year, Mann-comma-Mister.
Too good to be true? No. Too good to be LEGAL? Sure.
...
Flip on a light outside a door with a lock, that's a job?
For you it is.
Back up.
FNAK
Start again.

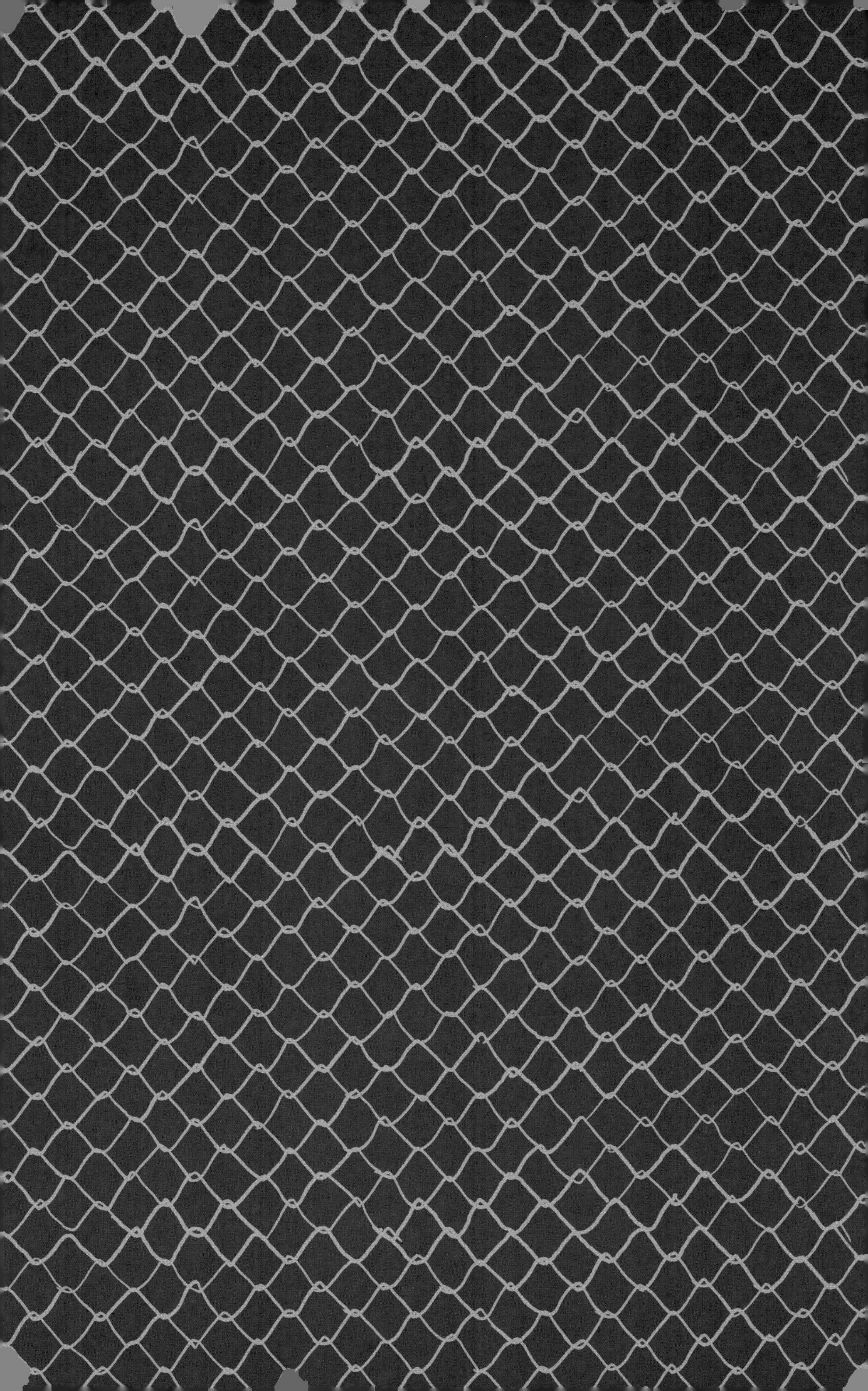

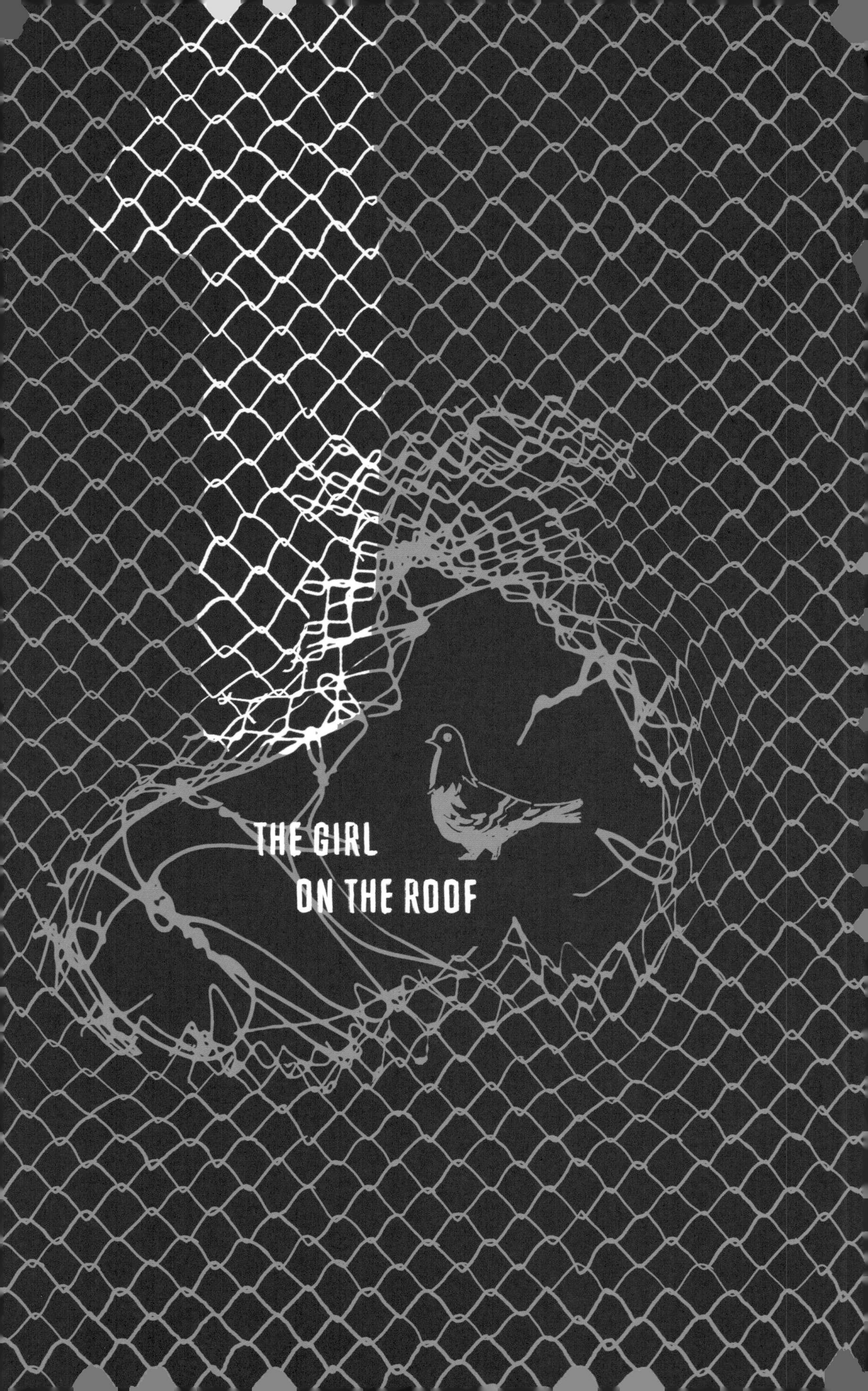
THE GIRL
ON THE ROOF

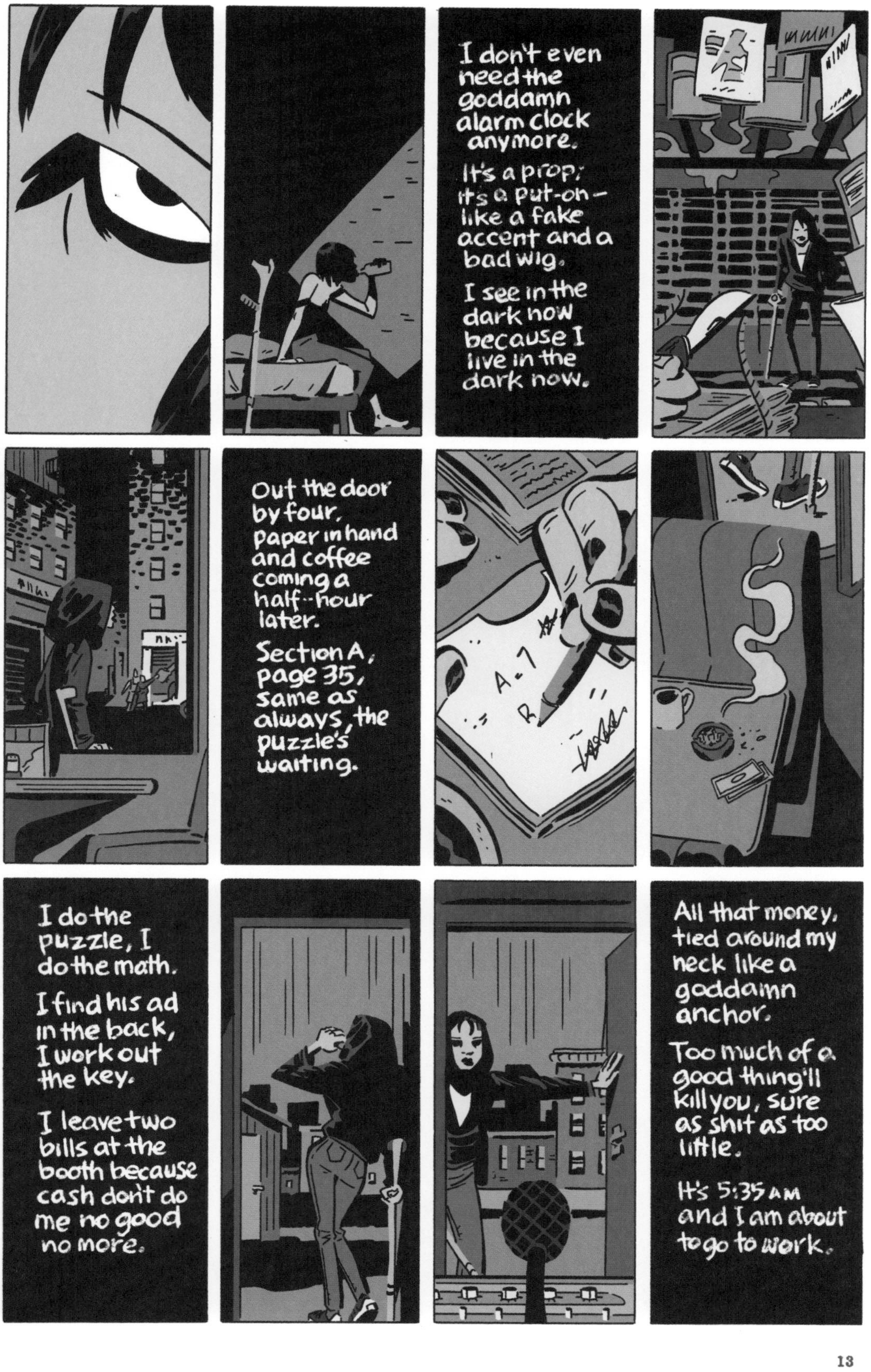
I don't even need the goddamn alarm clock anymore.
It's a prop; it's a put-on—like a fake accent and a bad wig.
I see in the dark now because I live in the dark now.
Out the door by four, paper in hand and coffee coming a half-hour later.
Section A, page 35, same as always, the puzzle's waiting.
I do the puzzle, I do the math.
I find his ad in the back, I work out the key.
I leave two bills at the booth because cash don't do me no good no more.
All that money, tied around my neck like a goddamn anchor.
Too much of a good thing'll kill you, sure as shit as too little.
It's 5:35 AM and I am about to go to work.

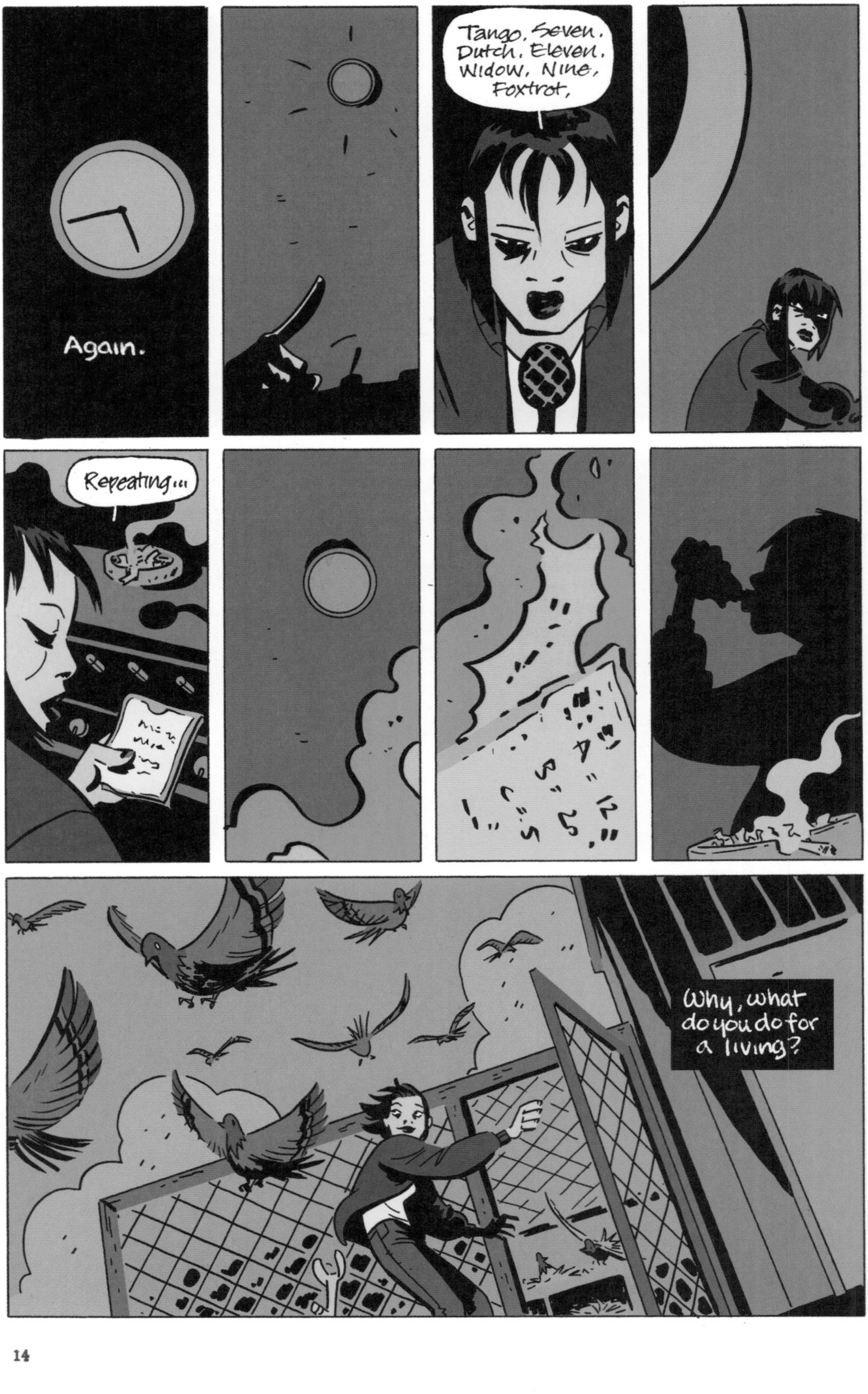
Again.
Tango, Seven, Dutch, Eleven, Widow, Nine, Foxtrot,
Repeating...
Why, what do you do for a living?

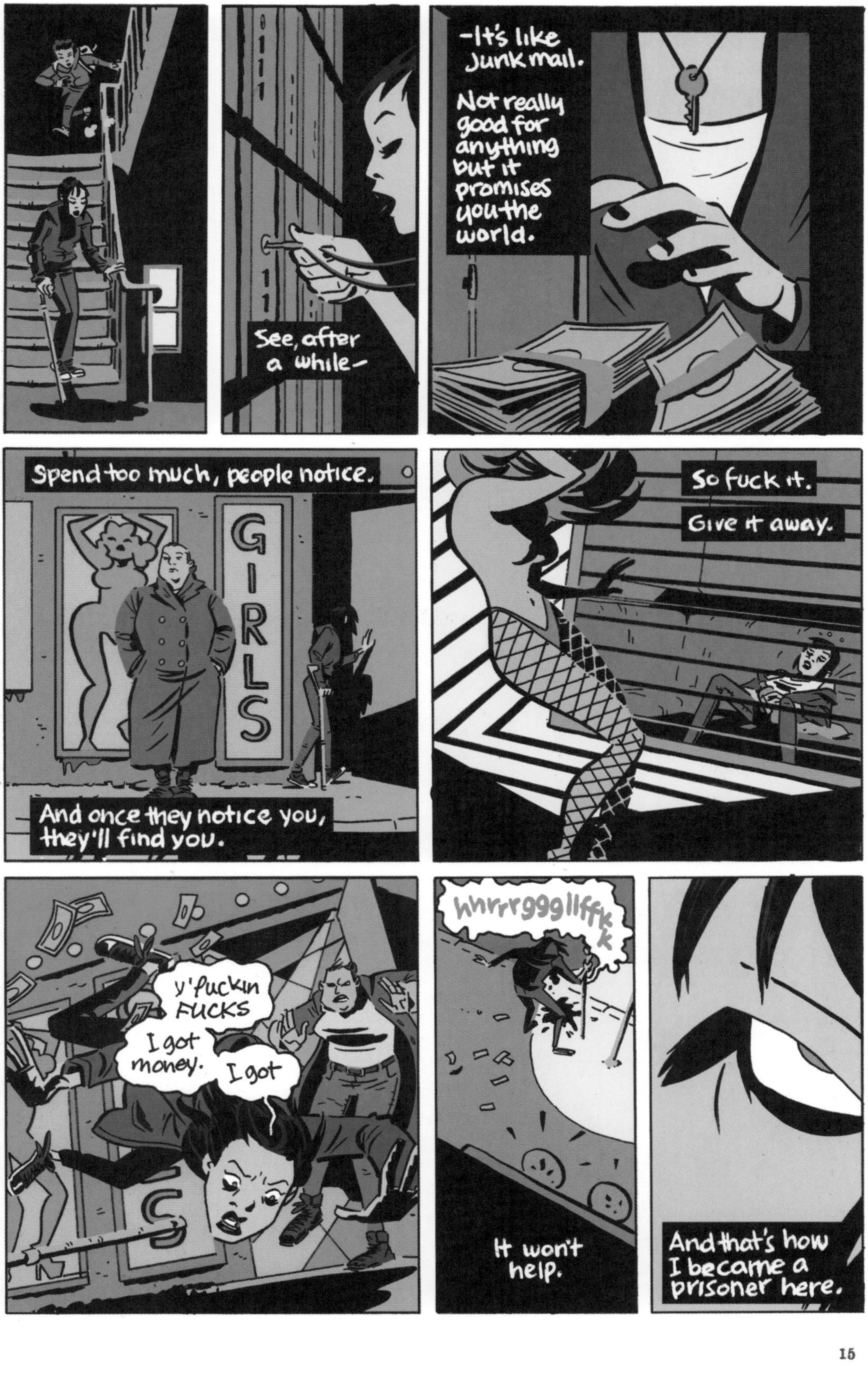
See, after a while-
-It's like Junk mail.
Not really good for anything but it promises you the world.
Spend too much, people notice.
GIRLS
And once they notice you, they'll find you.
So fuck it.
Give it away.
y'fuckin FUCKS
I got money.
I got
hhrrrggglllffkk
It won't help.
And that's how I became a prisoner here.

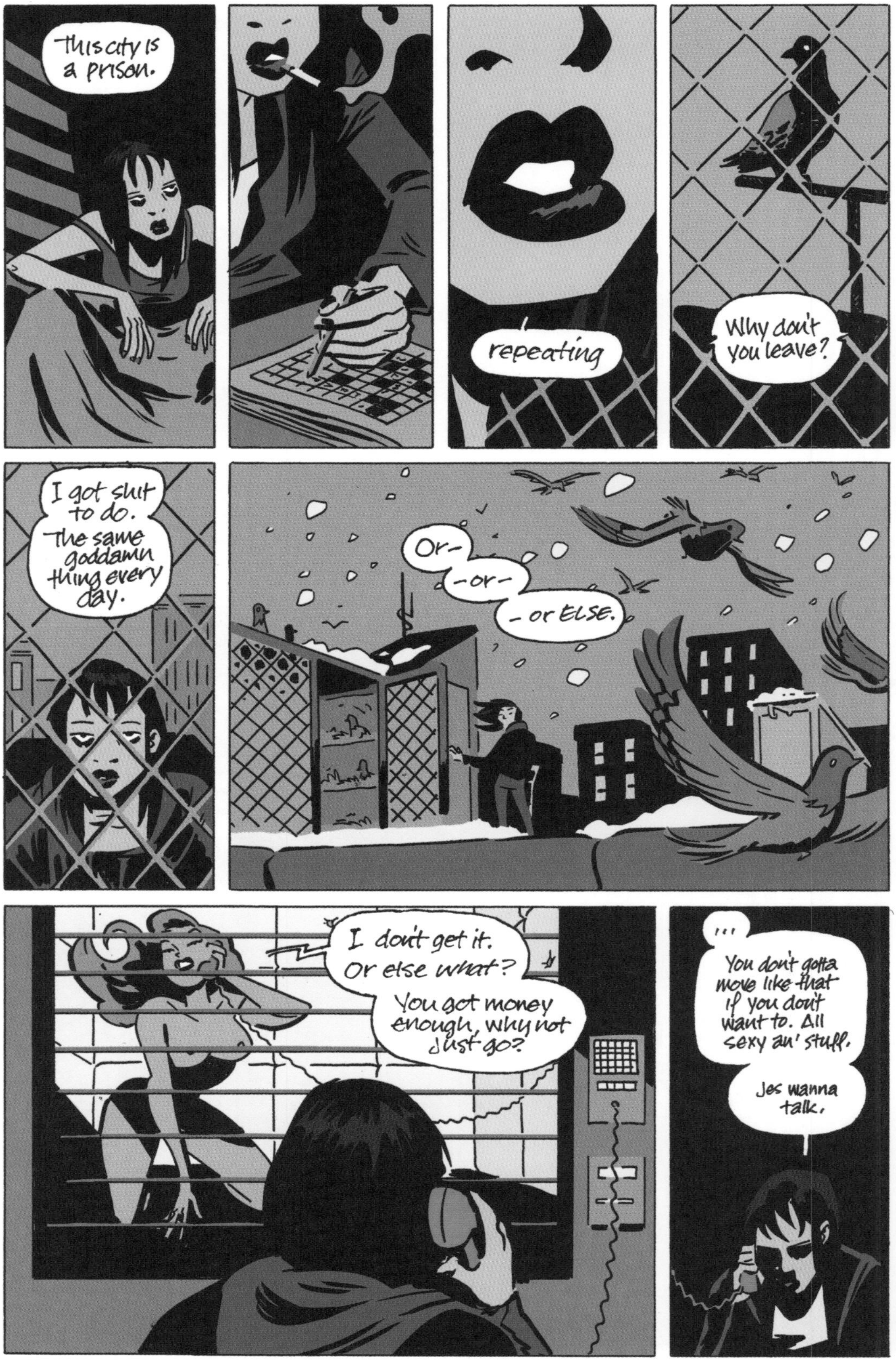
This city is a prison.
repeating
Why don't you leave?
I got shit to do. The same goddamn thing every day.
Or-
-or-
-or ELSE.
I don't get it. Or else what?
You got money enough, why not just go?
...
You don't gotta move like that if you don't want to. All sexy an' stuff.
Jes wanna talk.

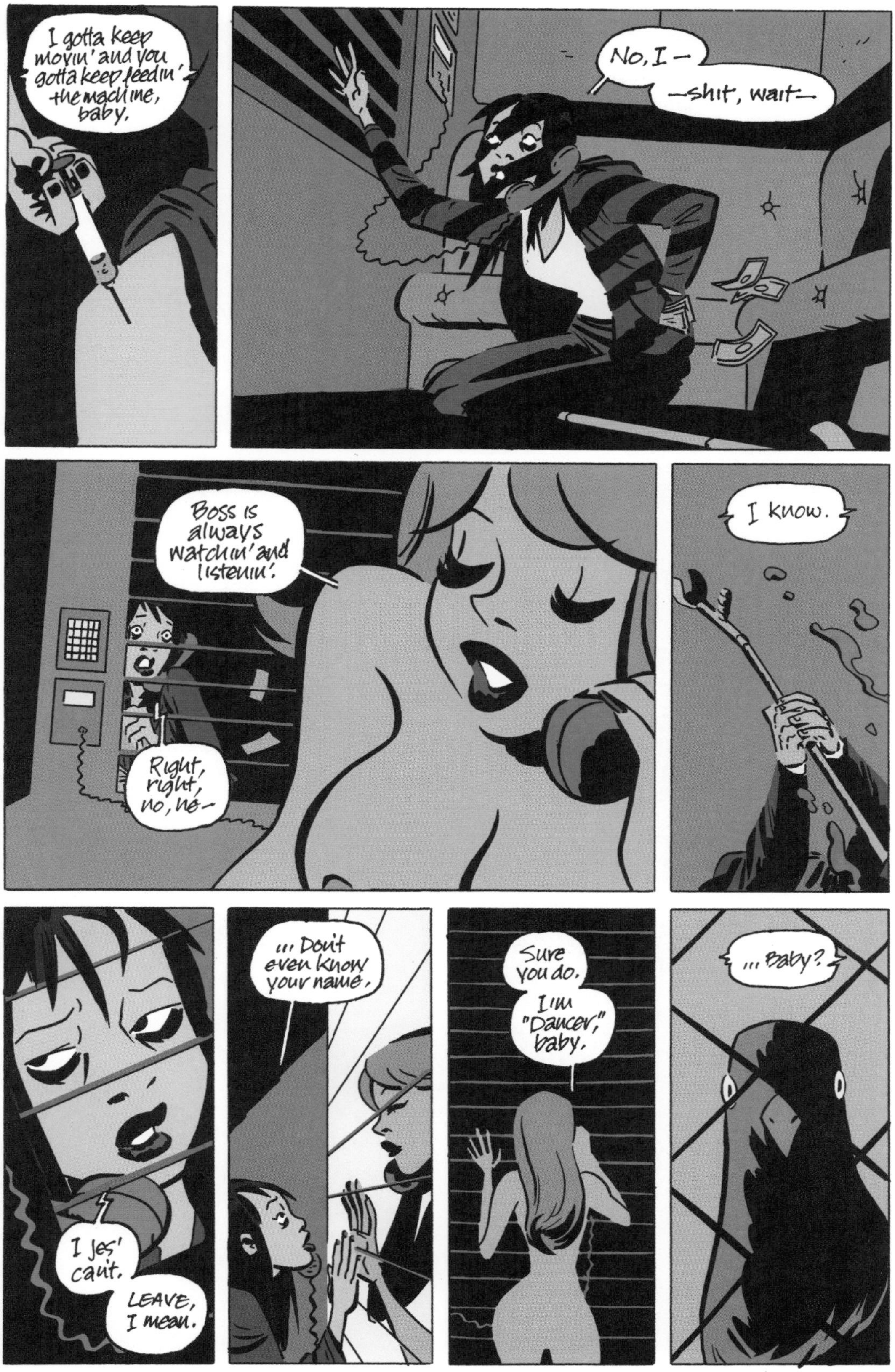
I gotta keep movin' and you gotta keep feedin' the machine, baby.
No, I—
—shit, wait—
Boss is always watchin' and listenin'.
Right, right, no, he—
I know.
I jes' can't.
LEAVE, I mean.
... Don't even know your name.
Sure you do.
I'm "Dancer," baby.
... Baby?

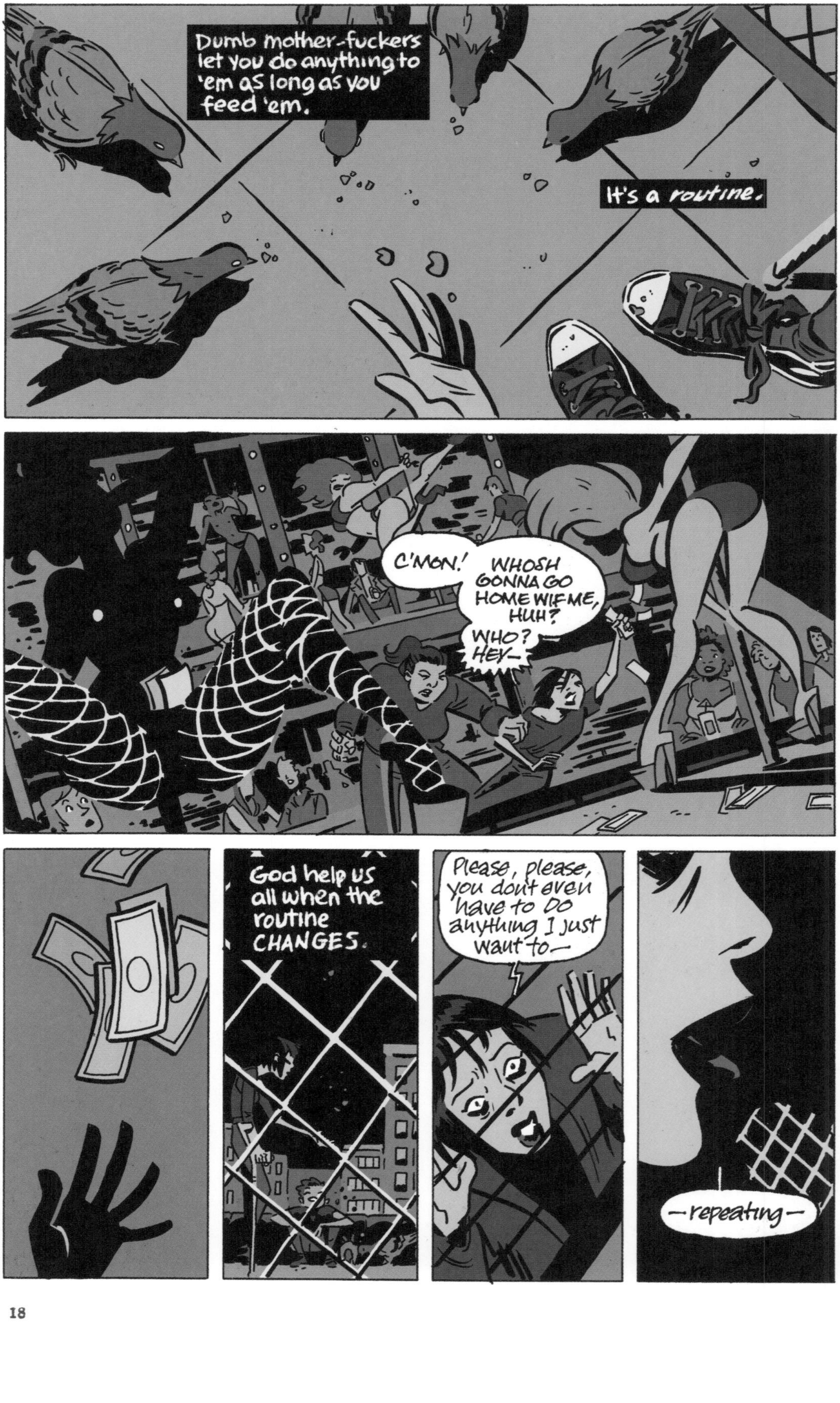
Dumb mother-fuckers let you do anything to 'em as long as you feed 'em.
It's a routine.
C'MON!
WHOSH GONNA GO HOME WIF ME, HUH?
WHO? HEY—
God help us all when the routine CHANGES.
Please, please, you don't even have to DO anything I just want to—
—repeating—

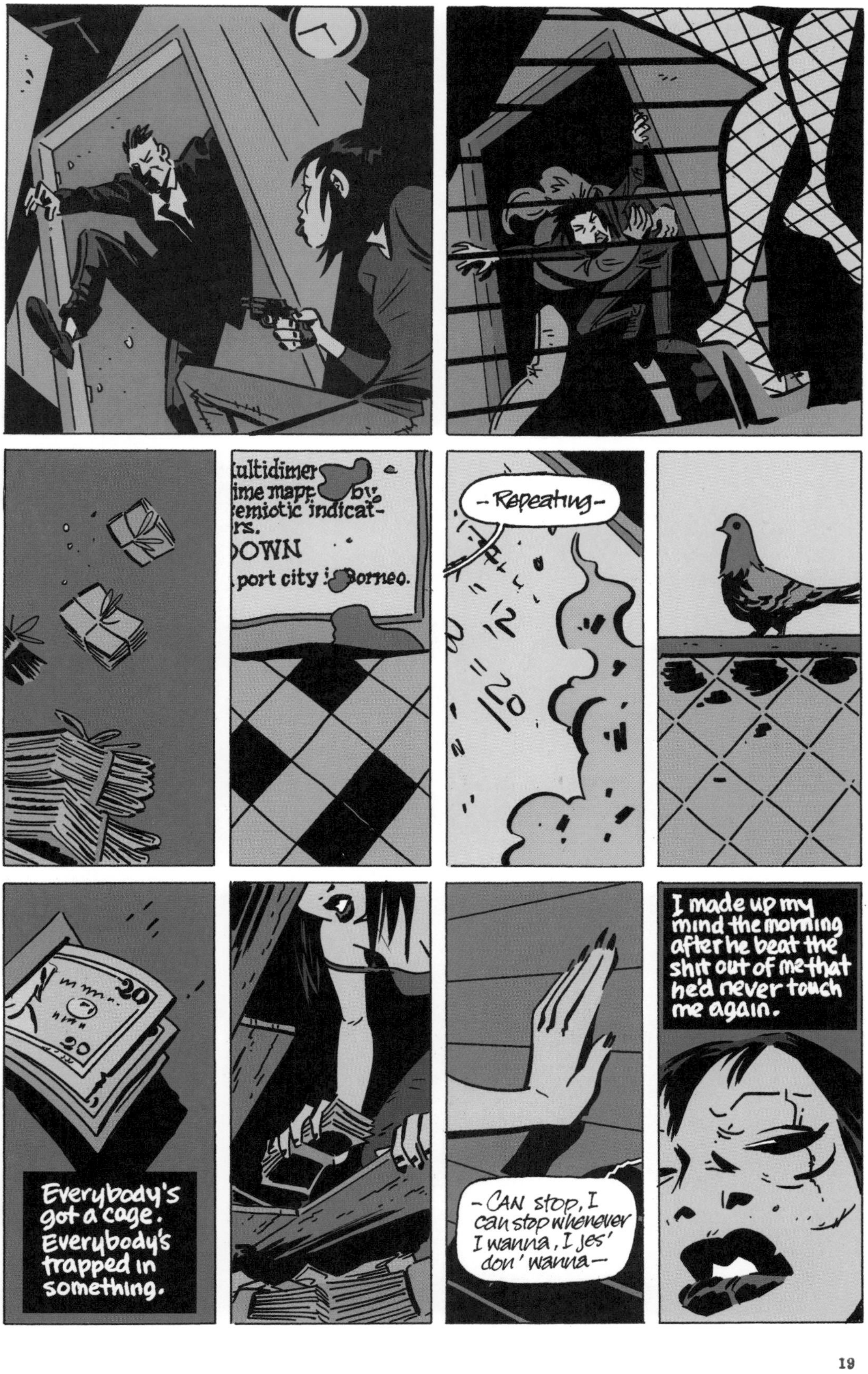

ultidimer
ime mapp by
emiotic indicat-
rs.
DOWN
port city Borneo.
-Repeating-
Everybody's got a cage. Everybody's trapped in something.
-CAN stop, I can stop whenever I wanna, I jes' don' wanna-
I made up my mind the morning after he beat the shit out of me that he'd never touch me again.

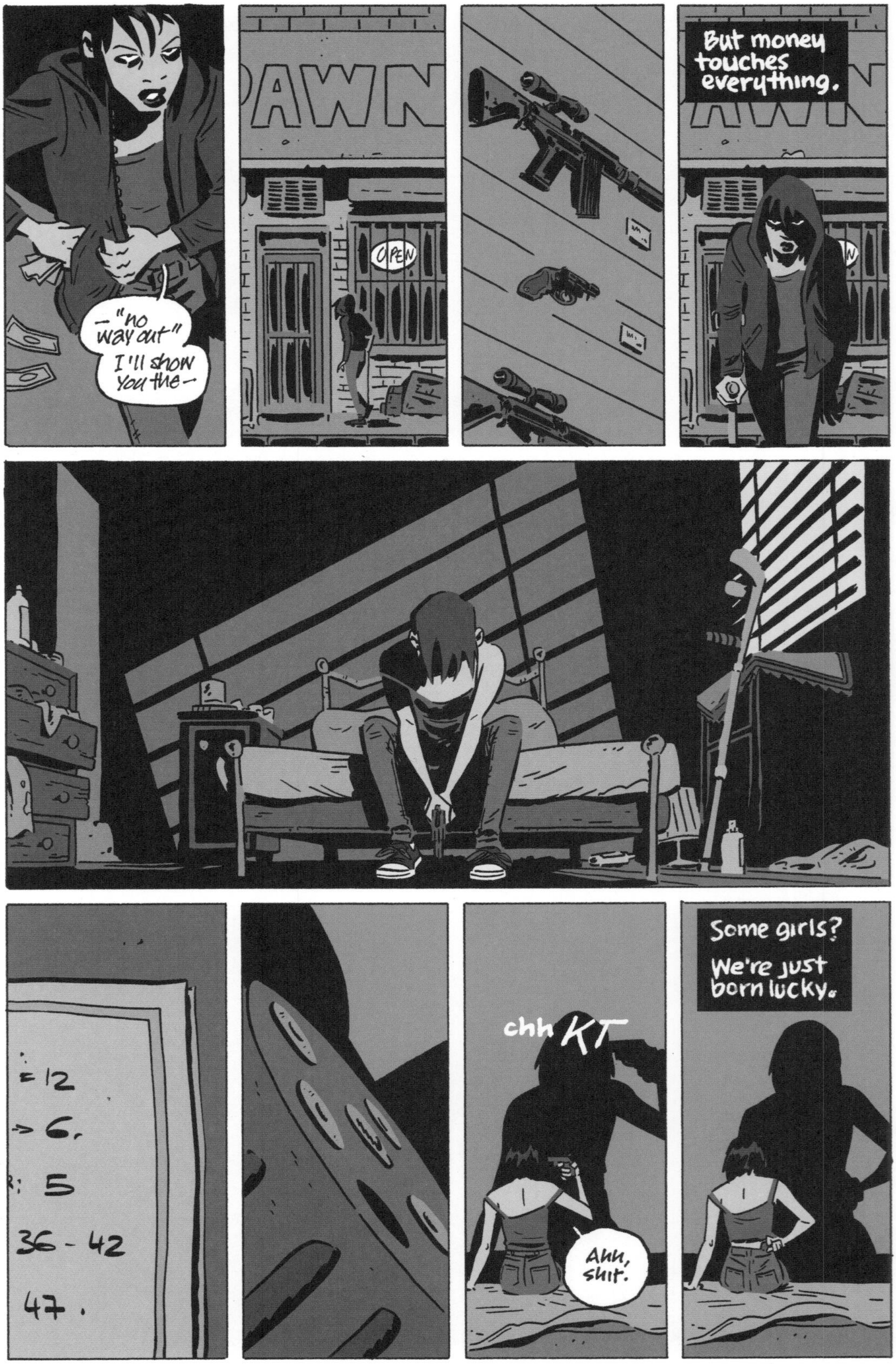
—"no way out" I'll show you the—
But money touches everything.
OPEN
PAWN
=12
→6.
: 5
36 - 42
47.
chh KT
Ahh, shit.
Some girls?
We're just born lucky.

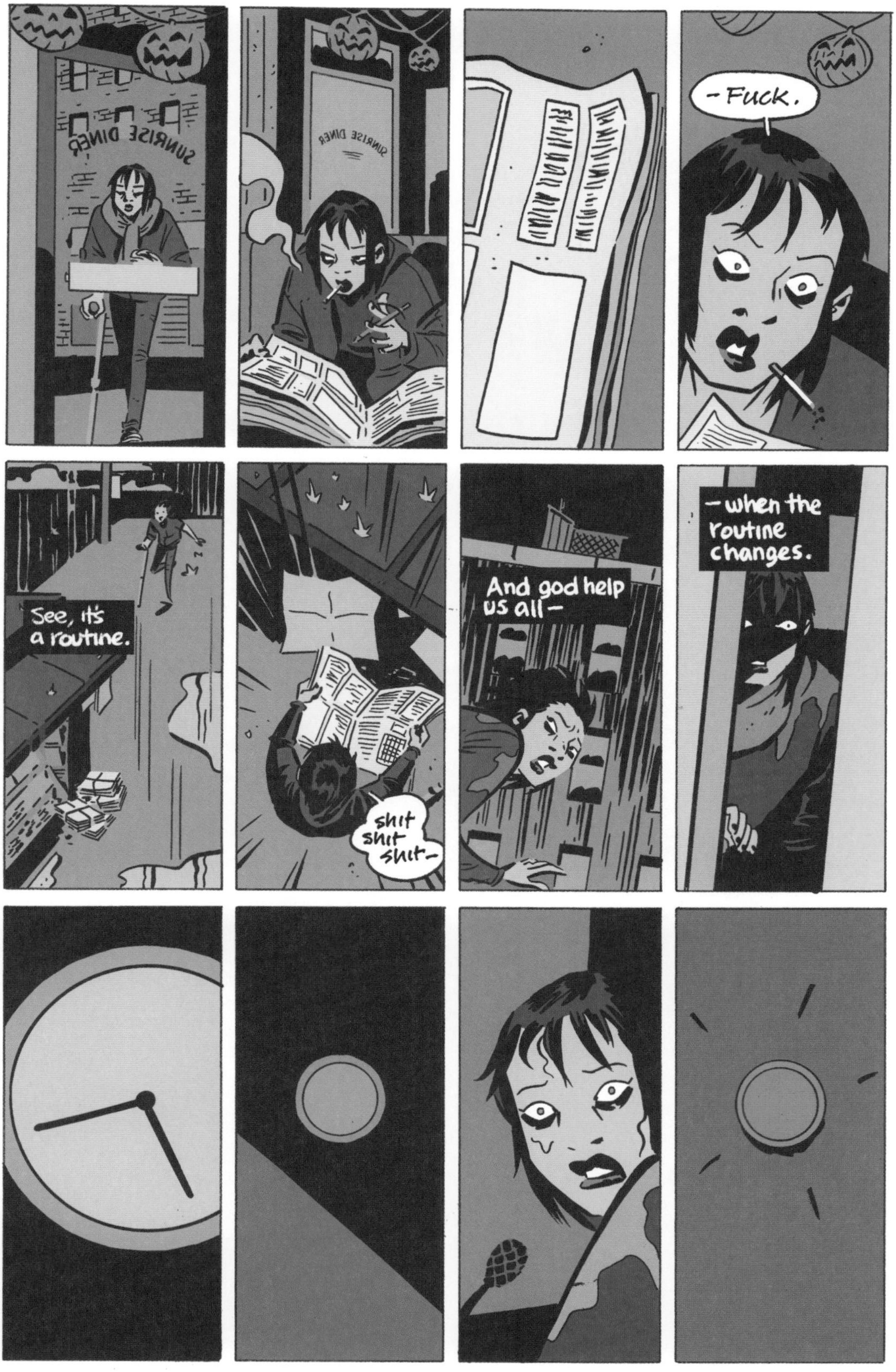
SUNRISE DINER
SUNRISE DINER
-Fuck.
See, it's a routine.
shit shit shit-
And god help us all-
-when the routine changes.

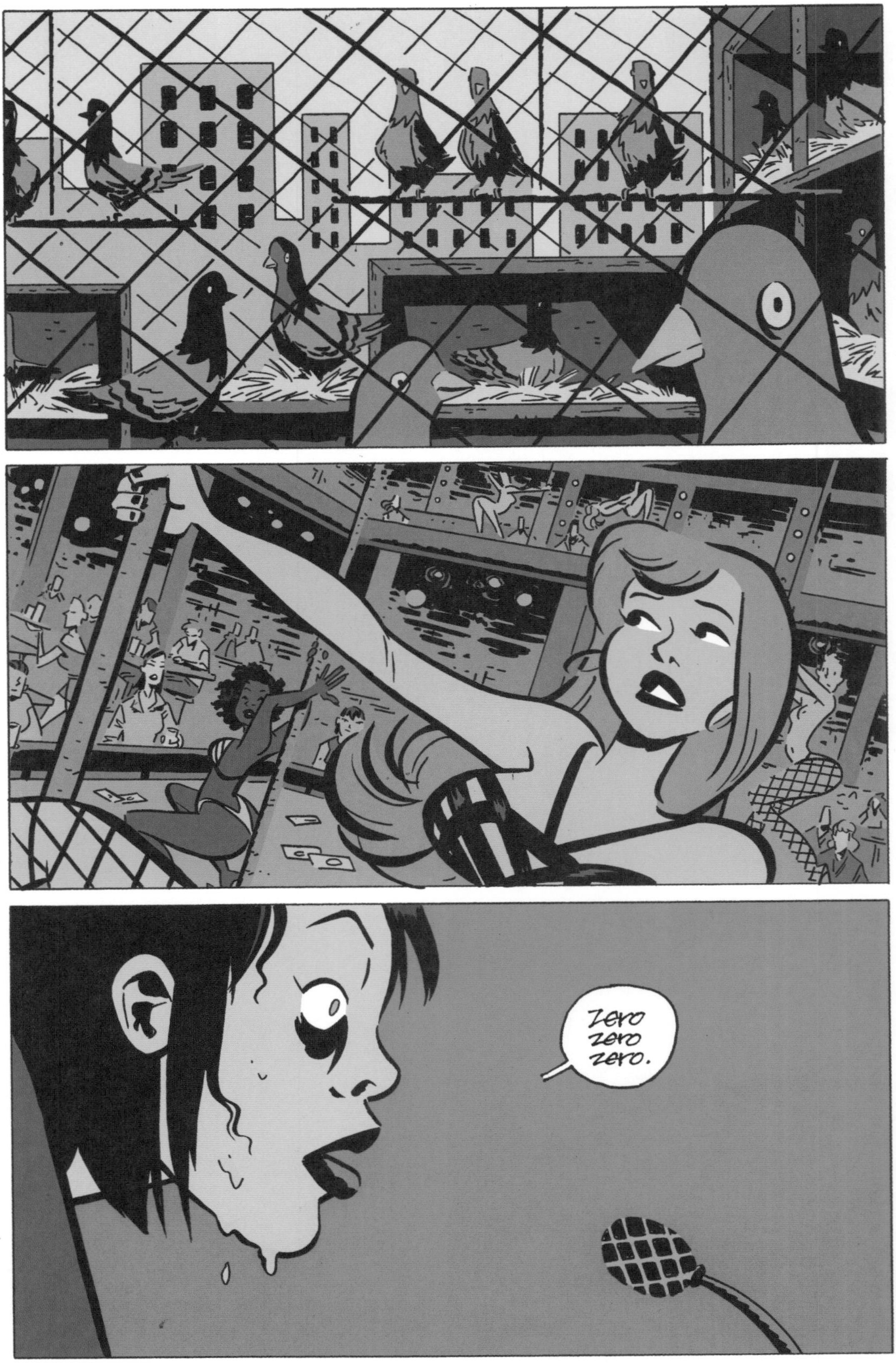
Zero zero zero.

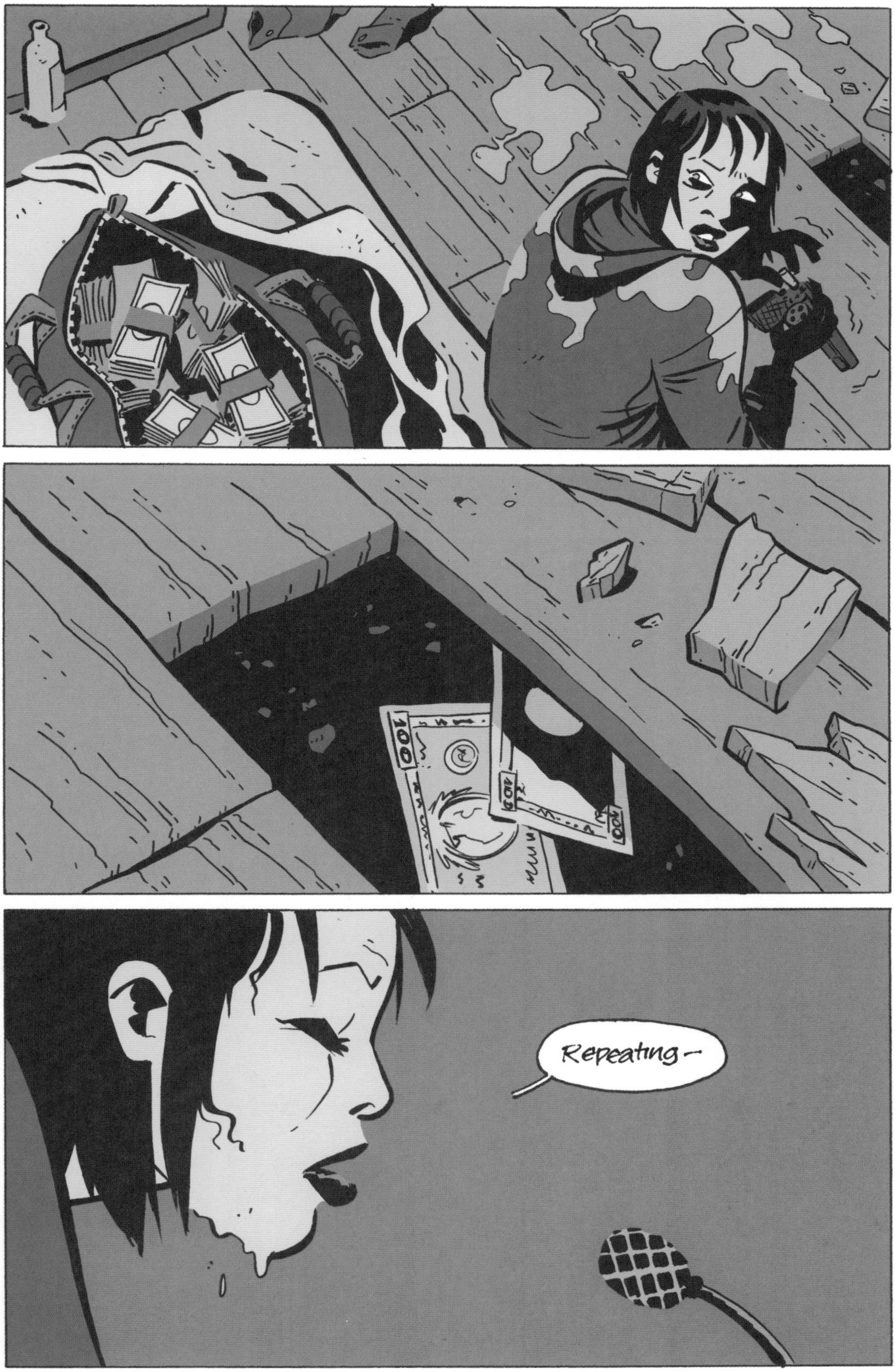
Repeating -

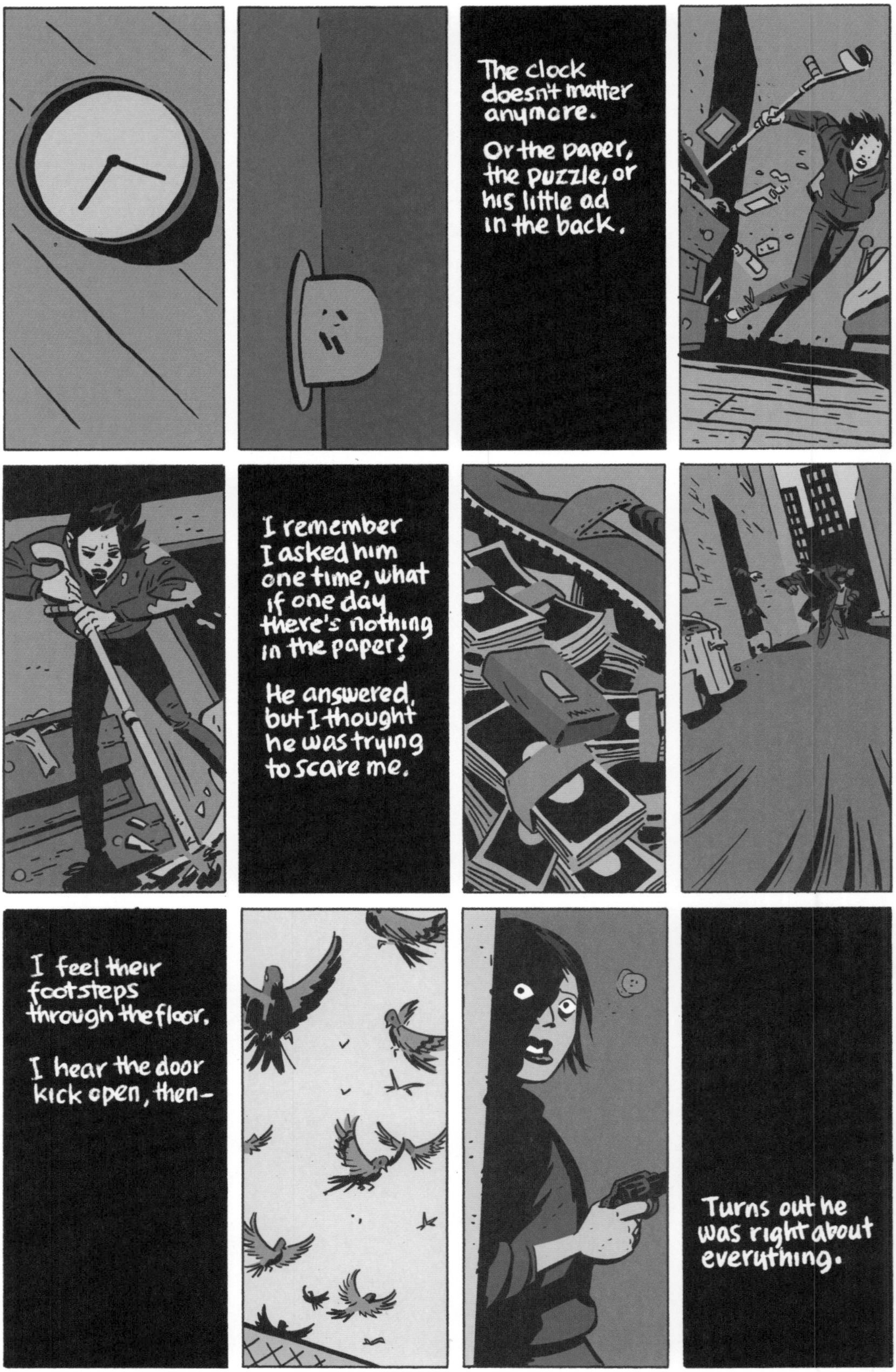
The clock doesn't matter anymore.
Or the paper, the puzzle, or his little ad in the back.
I remember I asked him one time, what if one day there's nothing in the paper?
He answered, but I thought he was trying to scare me.
I feel their footsteps through the floor.
I hear the door kick open, then-
Turns out he was right about everything.

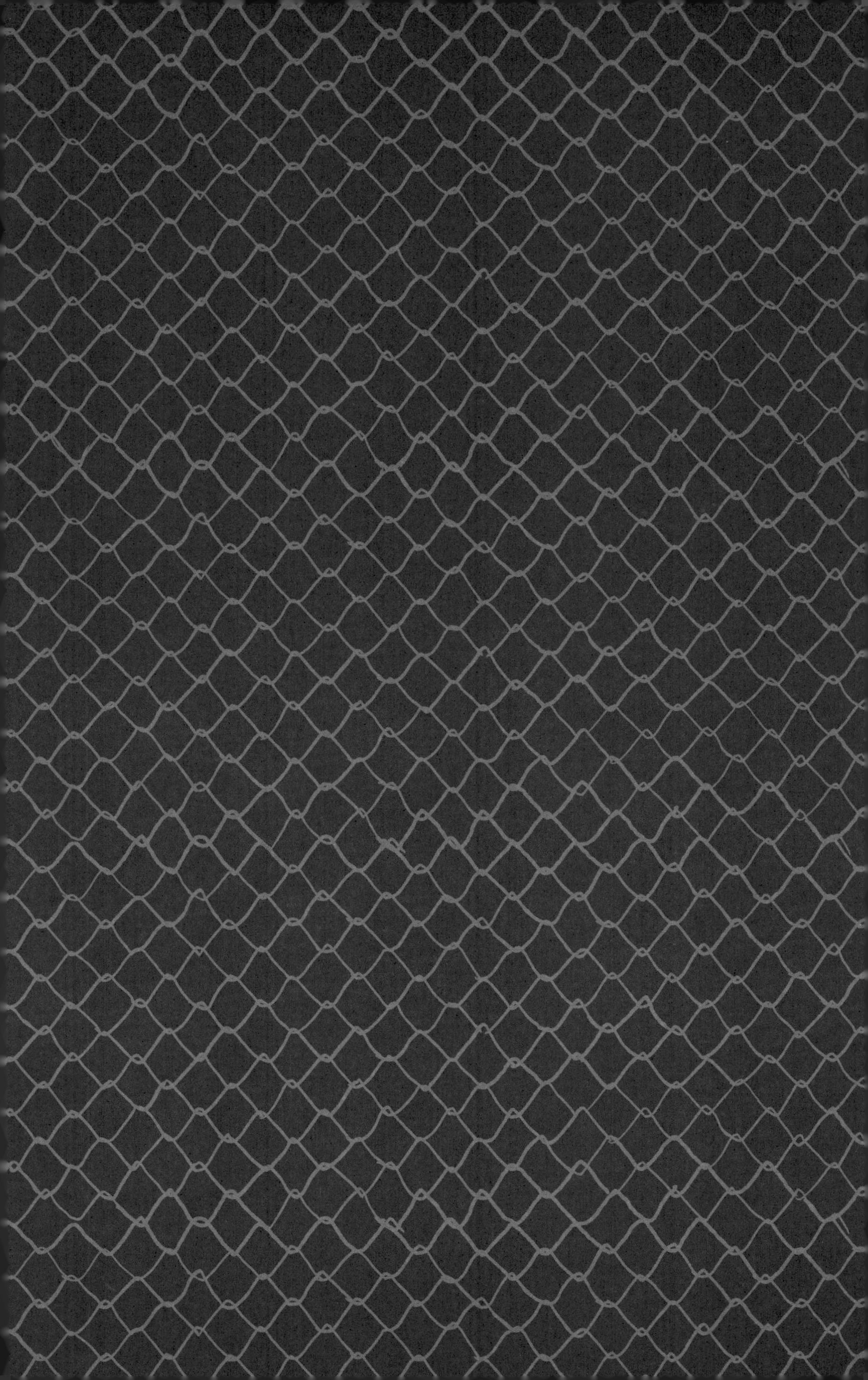

THE GUN IN THE PUDDLE

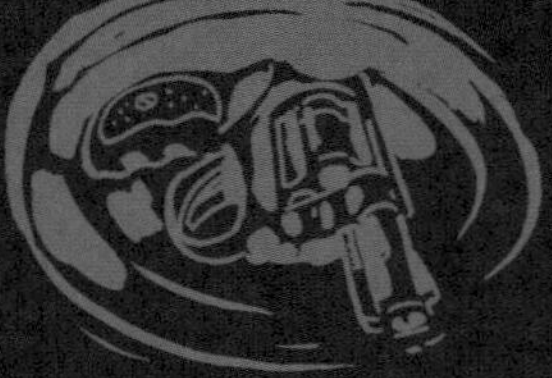

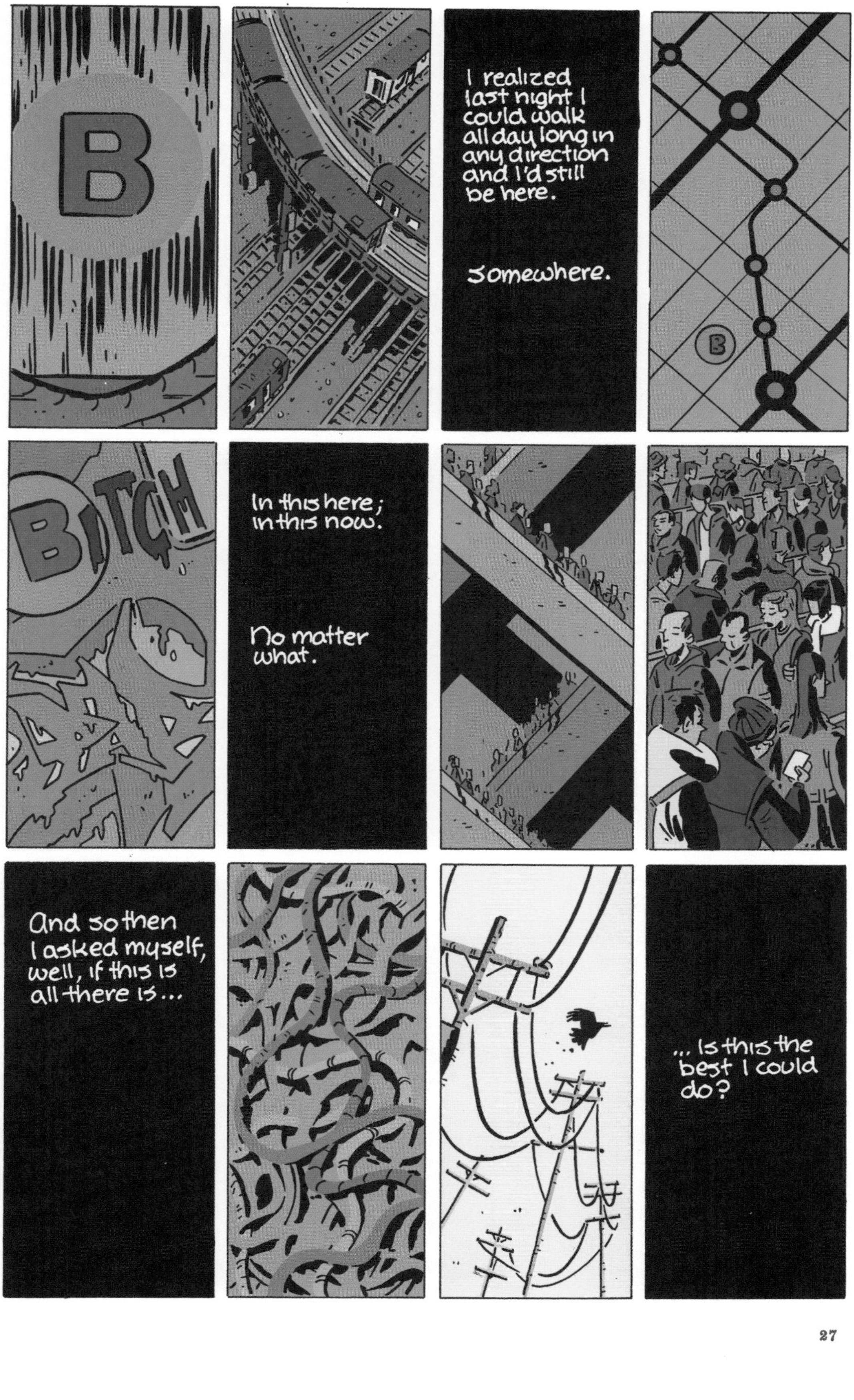
B
I realized last night I could walk all day long in any direction and I'd still be here.
Somewhere.
B
BITCH
In this here; in this now.
No matter what.
And so then I asked myself, well, if this is all there is...
... Is this the best I could do?

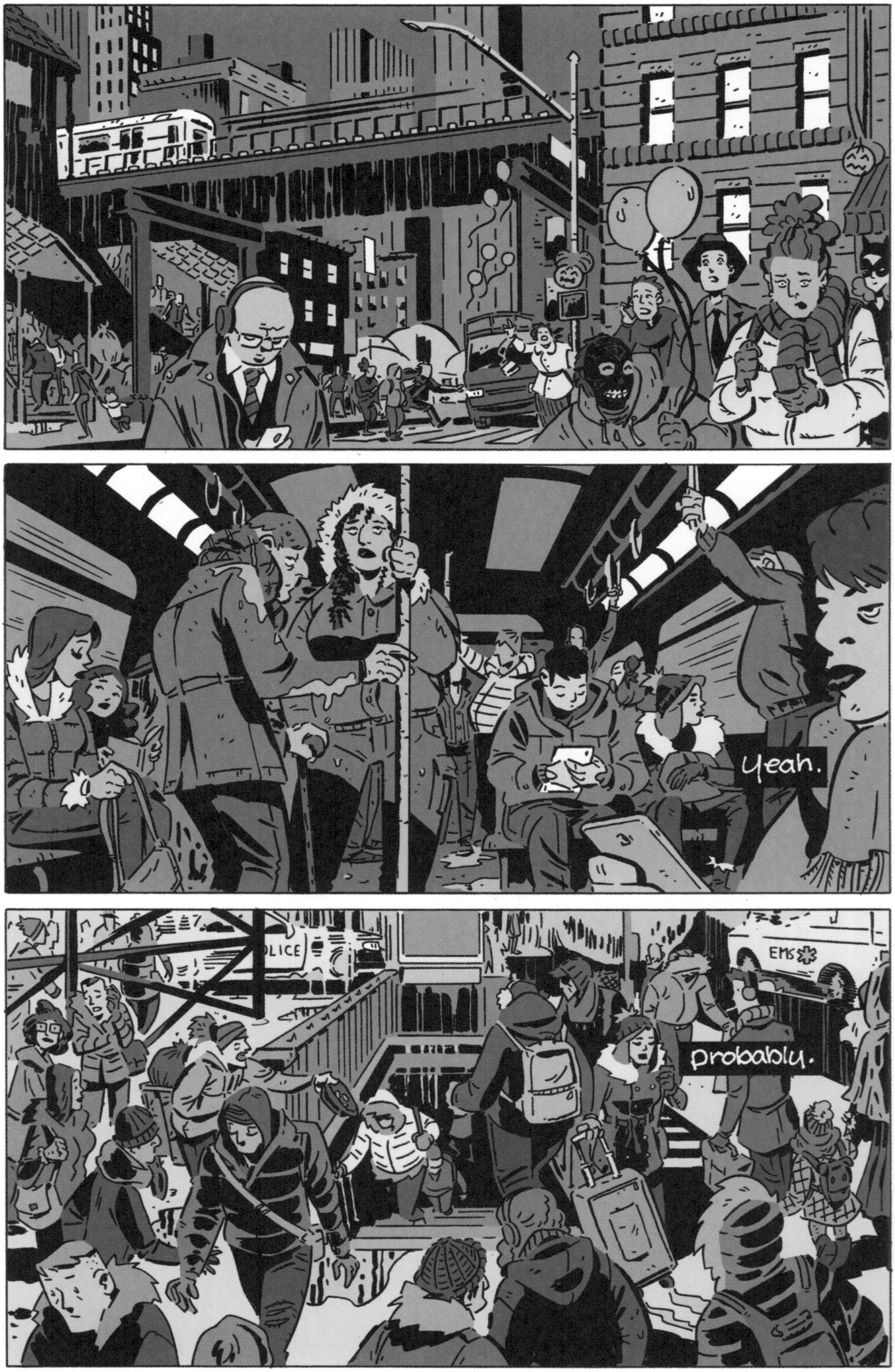
Yeah.
POLICE
EMS
probably.

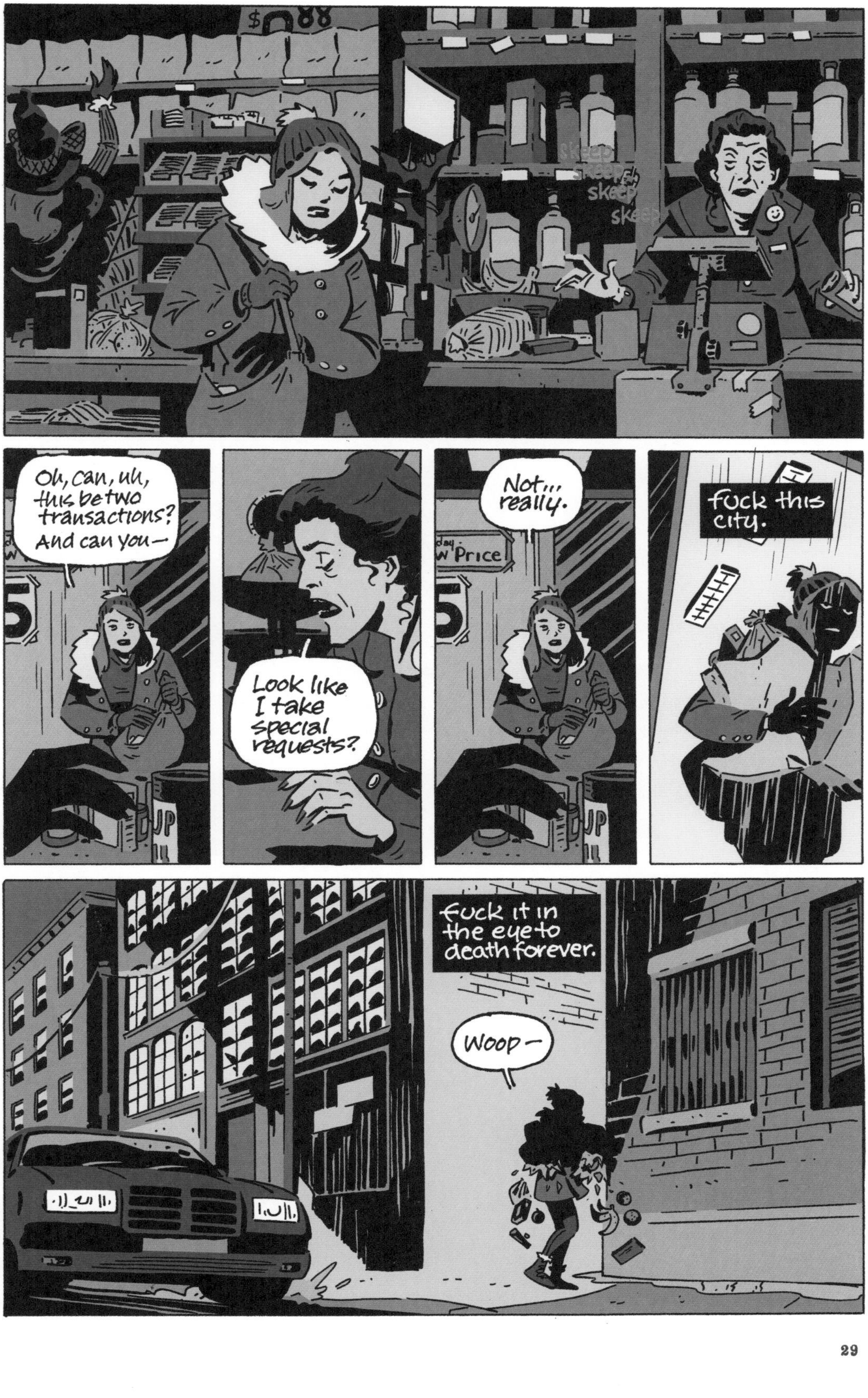

skeep skeep skeep skeep
Oh, can, uh, this be two transactions? And can you—
Look like I take special requests?
Not... really.
fuck this city.
fuck it in the eye to death forever.
Woop—

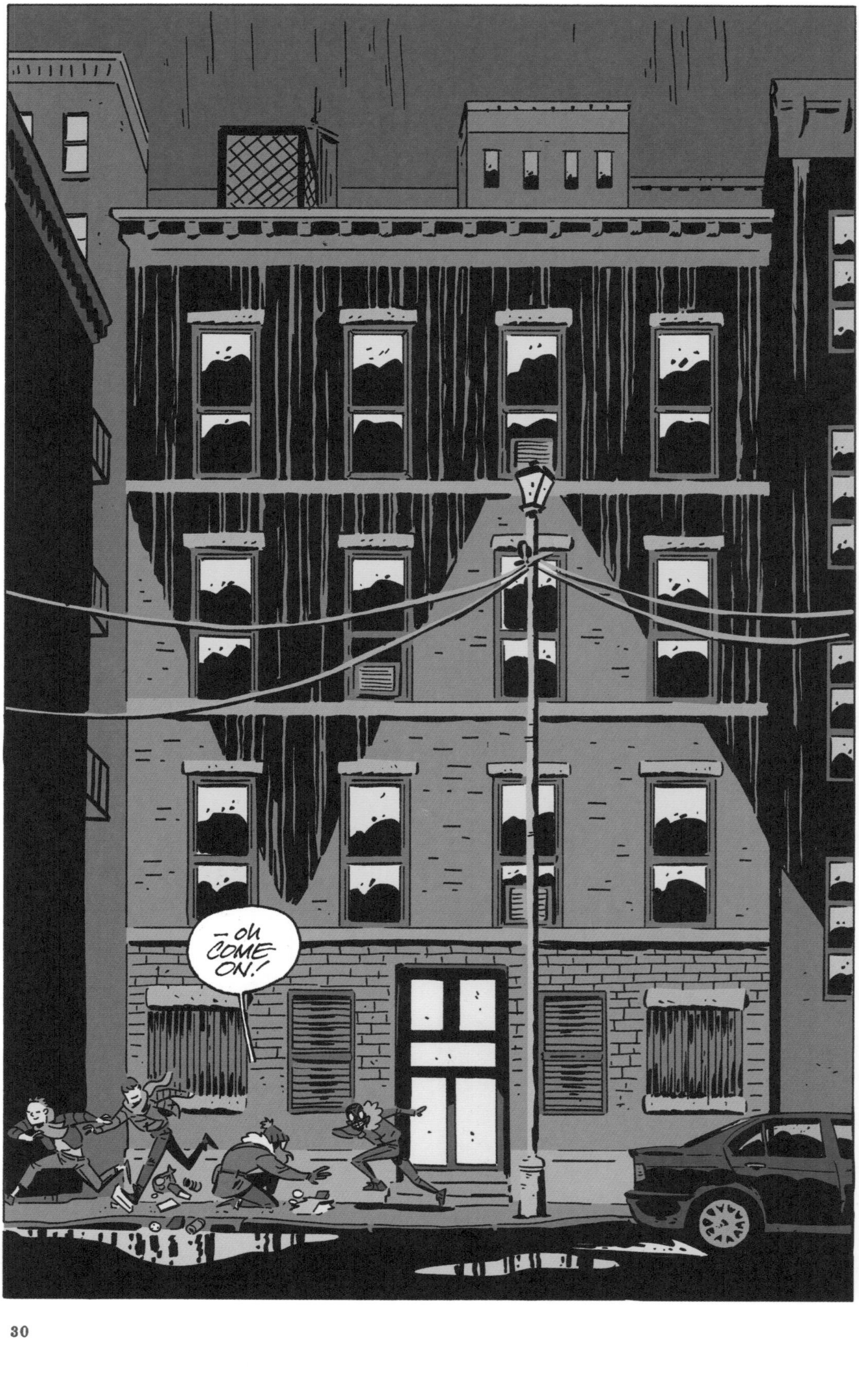
–OH COME ON.!

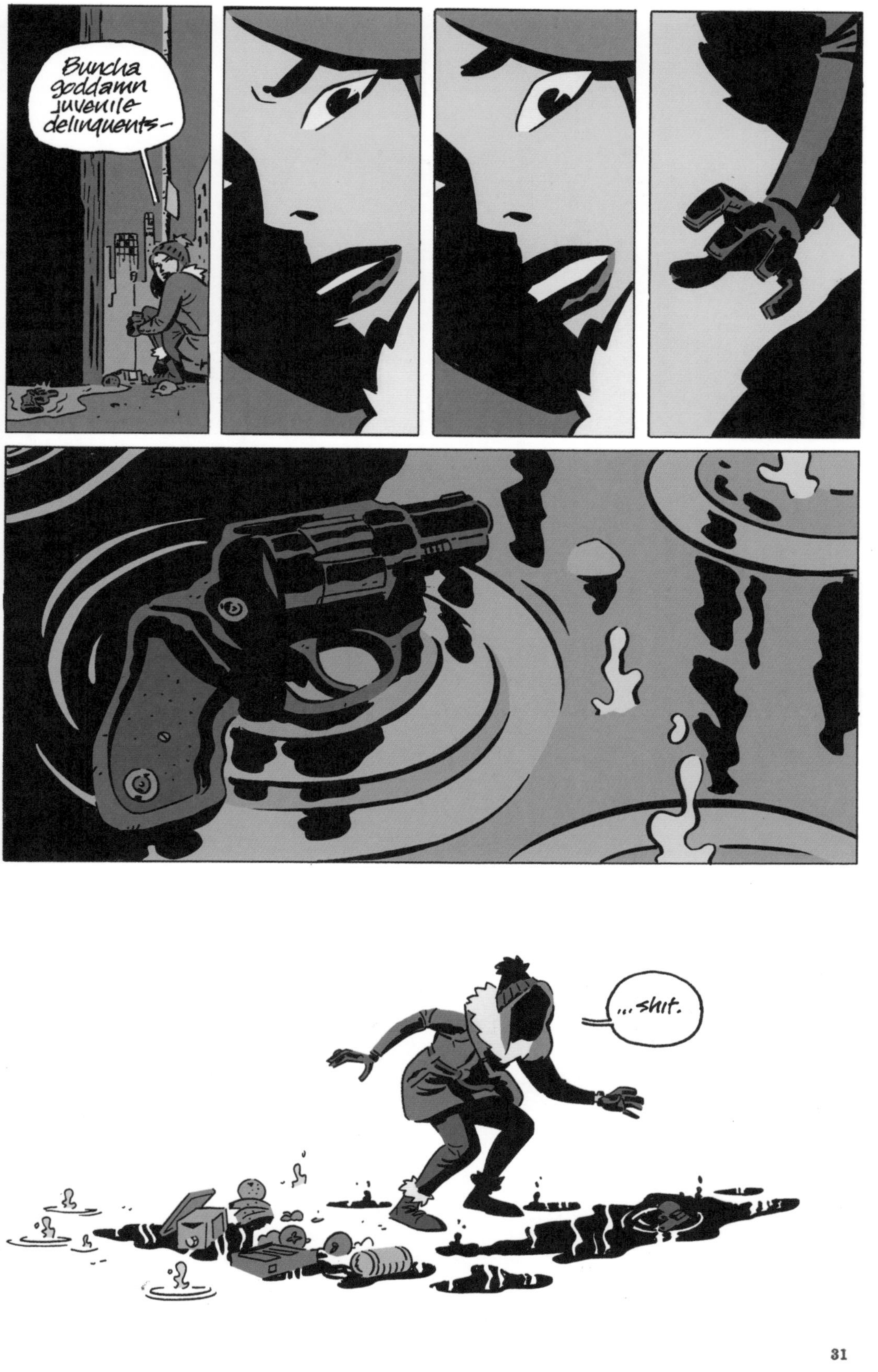
Buncha goddamn juvenile delinquents-
...shit.

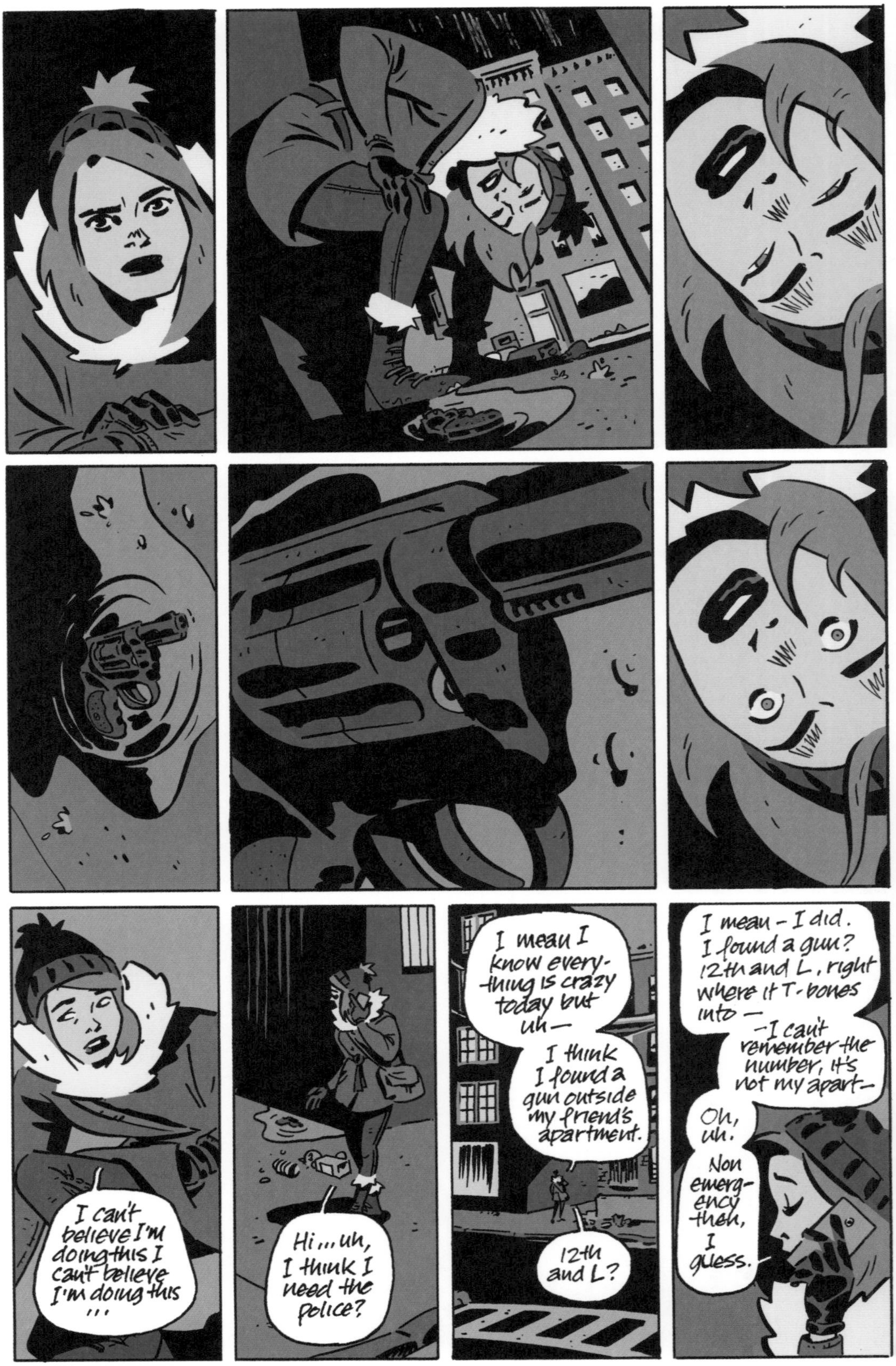
I can't believe I'm doing this I can't believe I'm doing this ...
Hi... uh, I think I need the police?
I mean I know every-thing is crazy today but uh—
I think I found a gun outside my friend's apartment.
12th and L?
I mean - I did. I found a gun? 12th and L, right where it T-bones into—
—I can't remember the number, it's not my apart—
Oh, uh.
Non emerg-ency then, I guess.

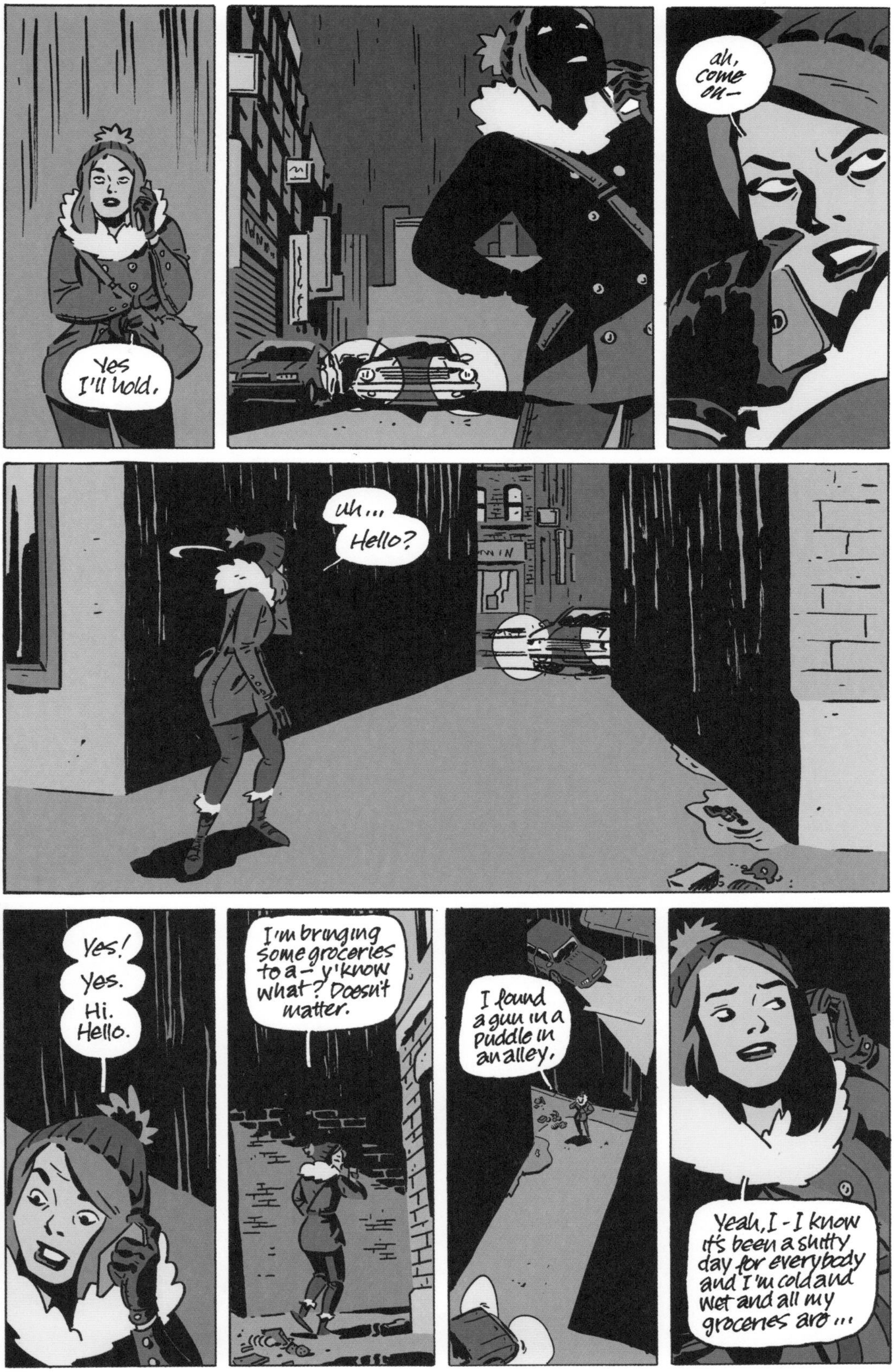
Yes I'll hold.
ah, come on—
uh... Hello?
Yes! Yes. Hi. Hello.
I'm bringing some groceries to a— y'know what? Doesn't matter.
I found a gun in a puddle in an alley.
Yeah, I - I know it's been a shitty day for everybody and I'm cold and wet and all my groceries are...

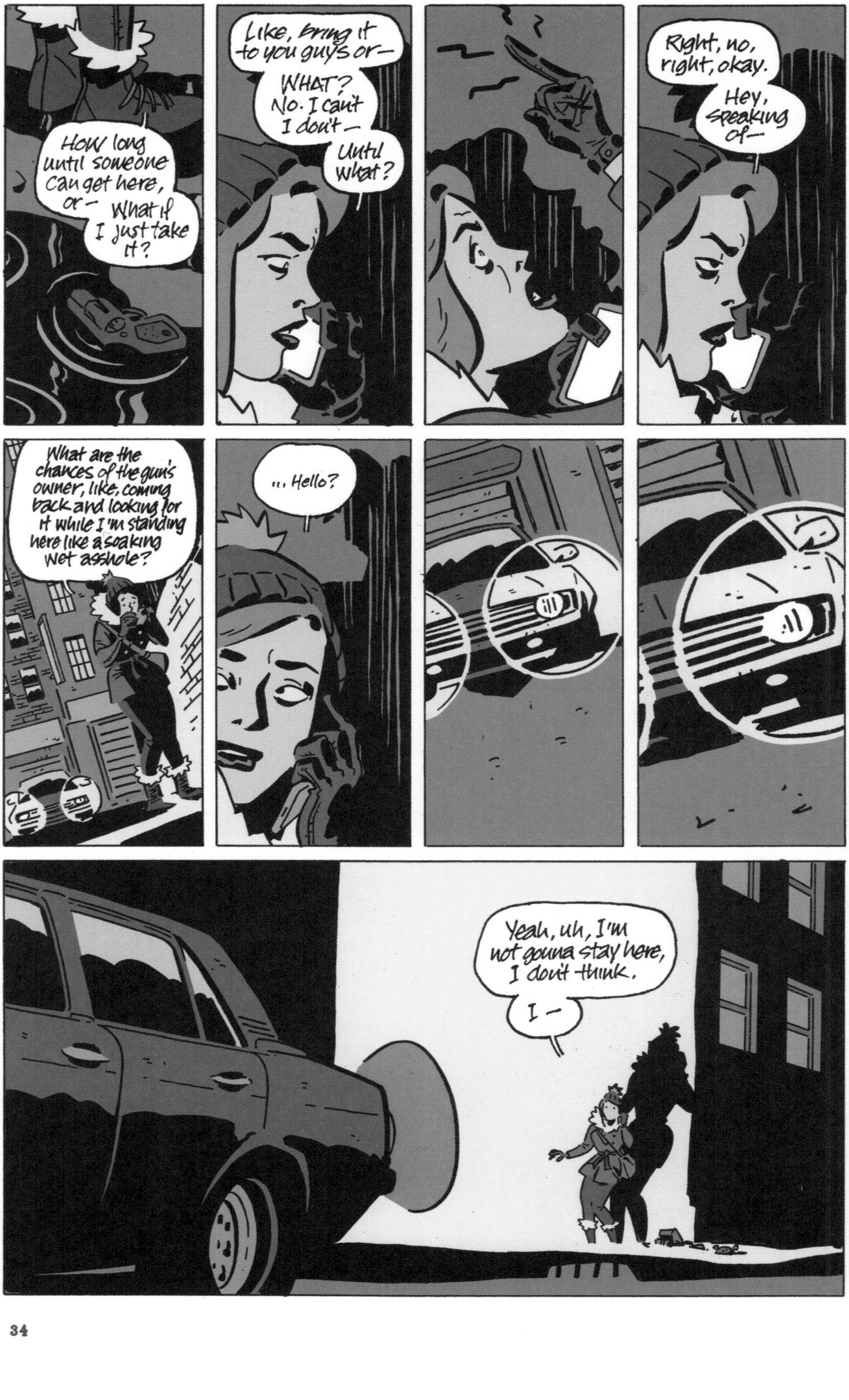
How long until someone can get here, or—
What if I just take it?
Like, bring it to you guys or—
WHAT? No. I can't I don't—
Until what?
Right, no, right, okay.
Hey, speaking of—
What are the chances of the gun's owner, like, coming back and looking for it while I'm standing here like a soaking wet asshole?
... Hello?
Yeah, uh, I'm not gonna stay here, I don't think.
I—

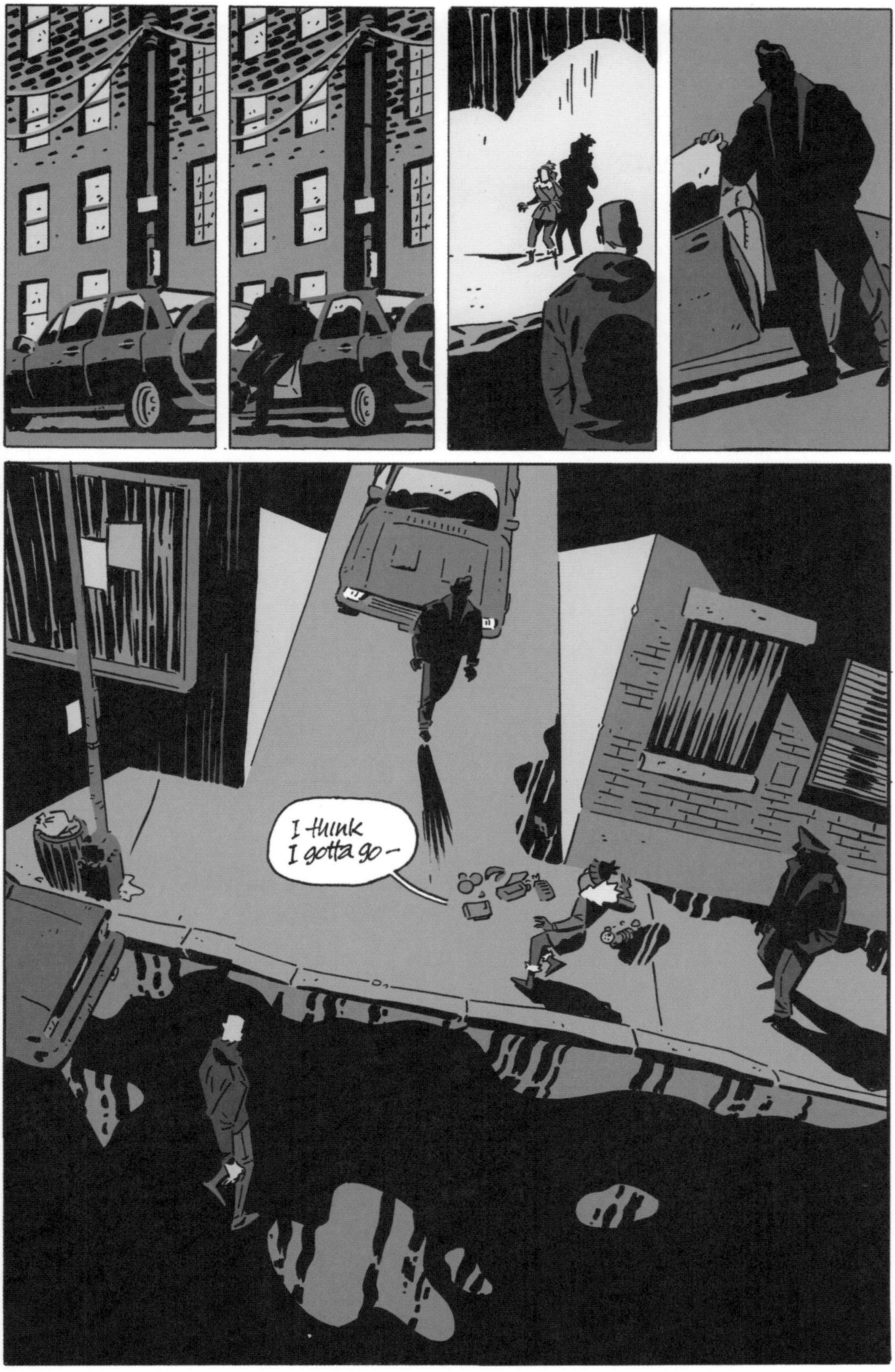
I think I gotta go-

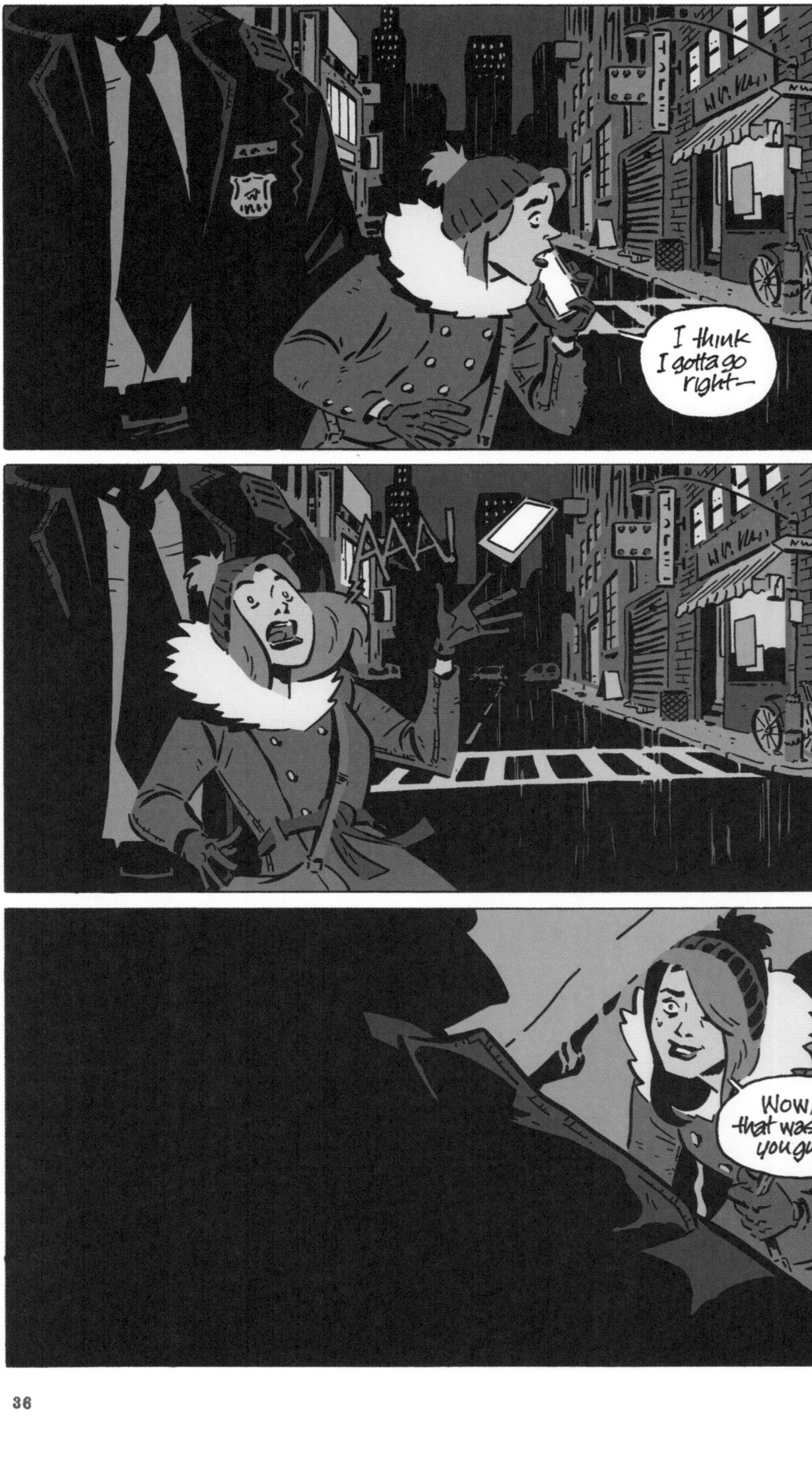
I think I gotta go right—
AAA!
Wow, that was fast, you guys—

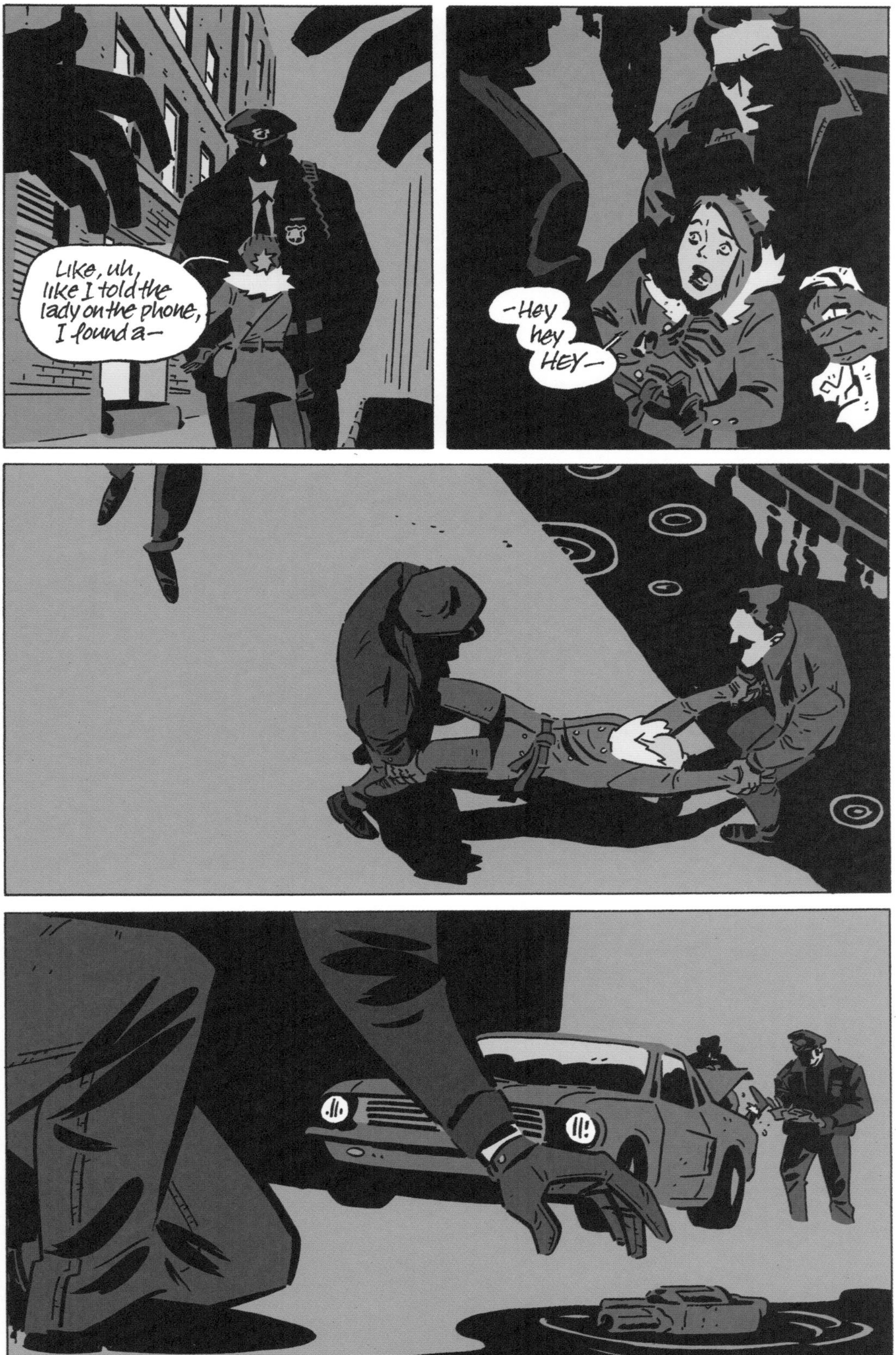
Like, uh, like I told the lady on the phone, I found a—
—Hey hey HEY—

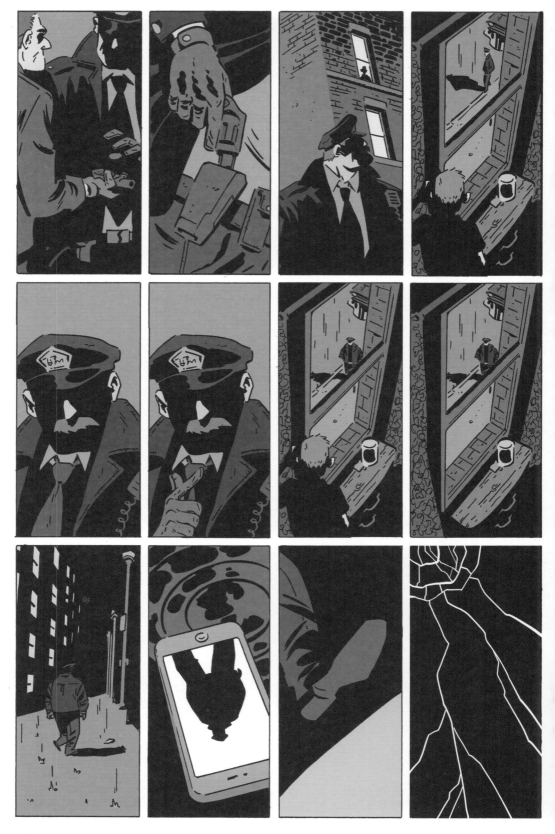

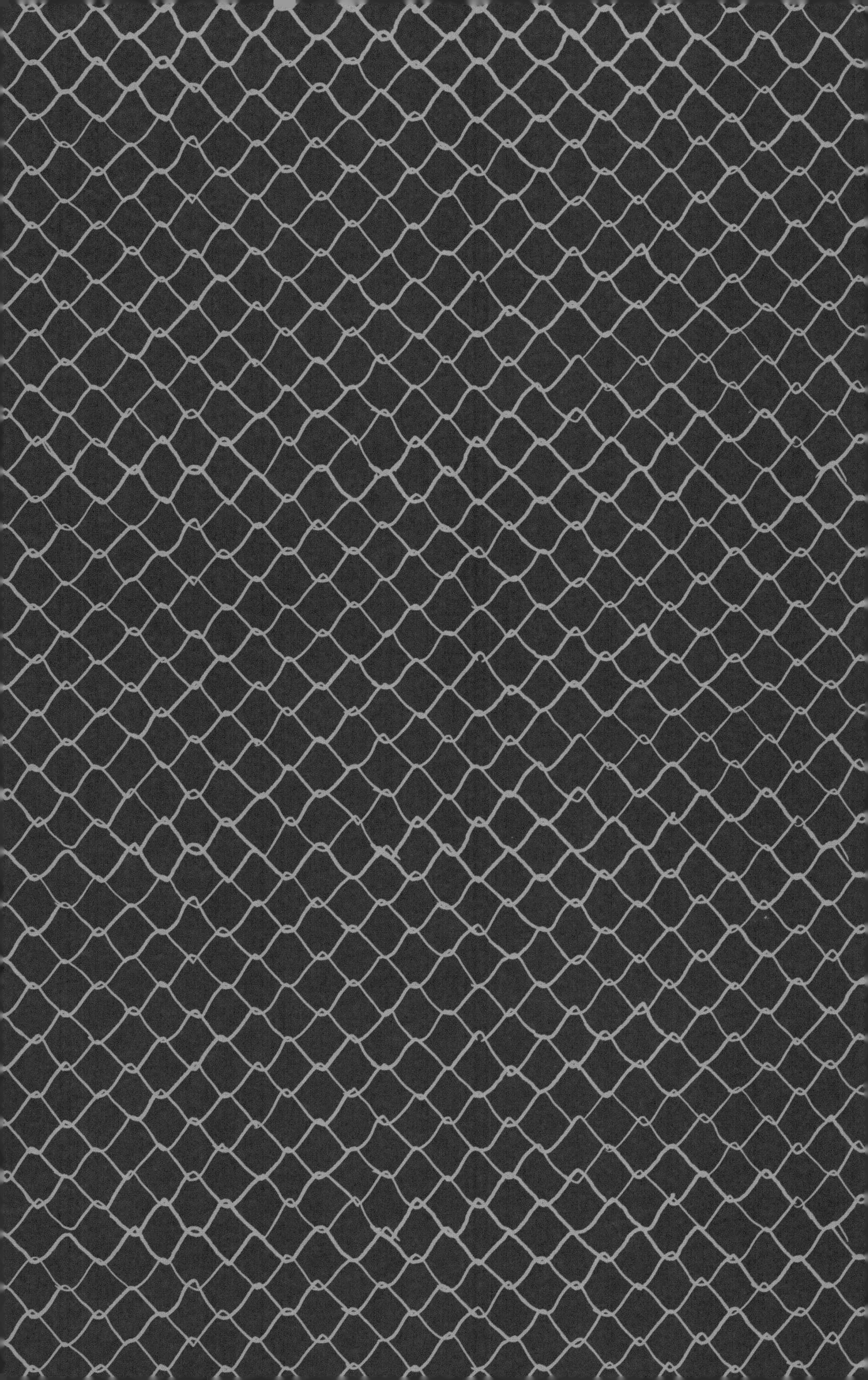

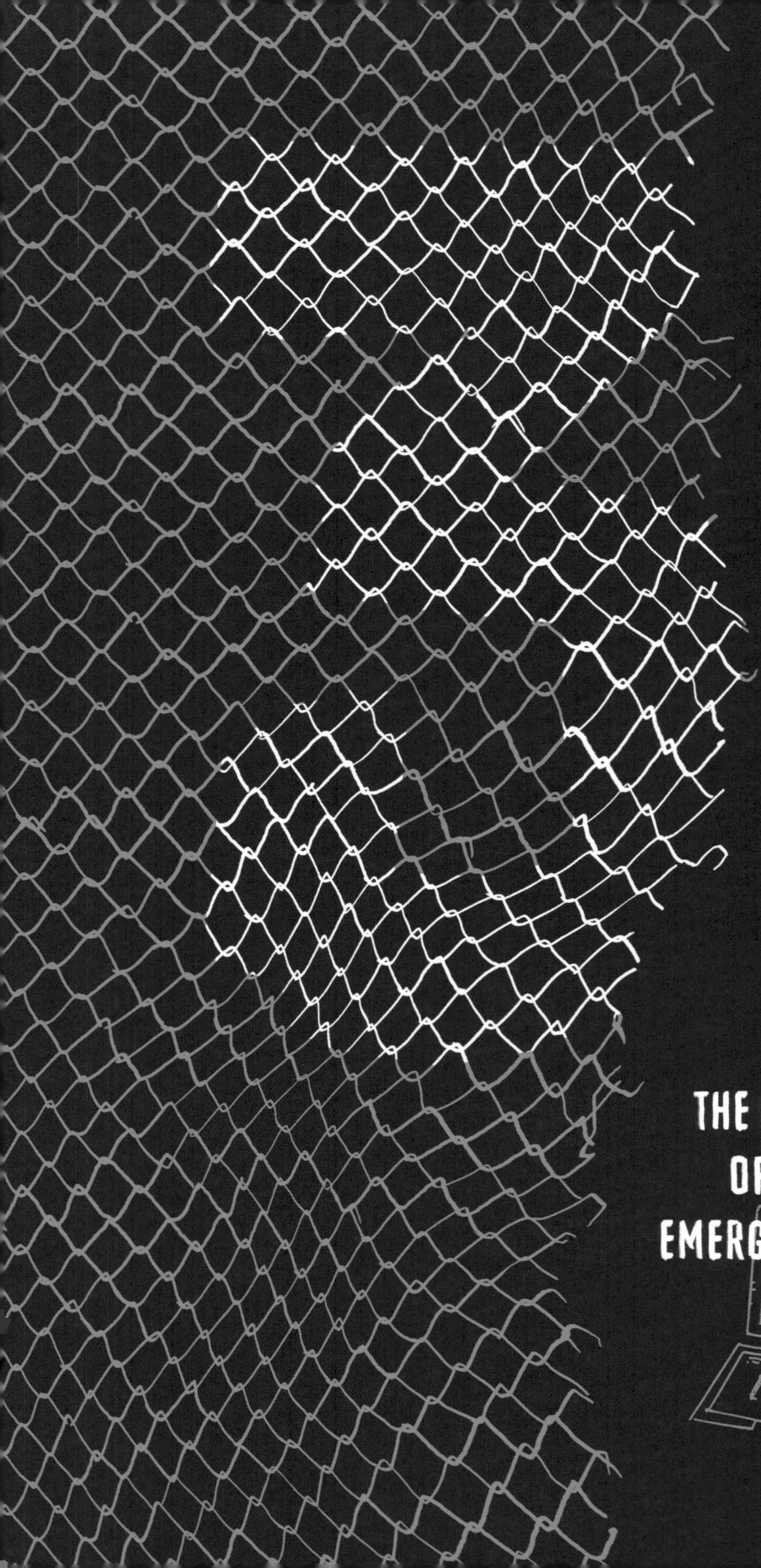

THE NATURE OF THE EMERGENCY

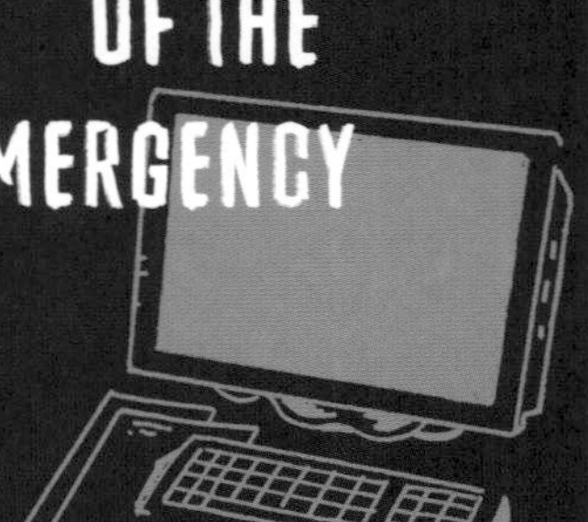

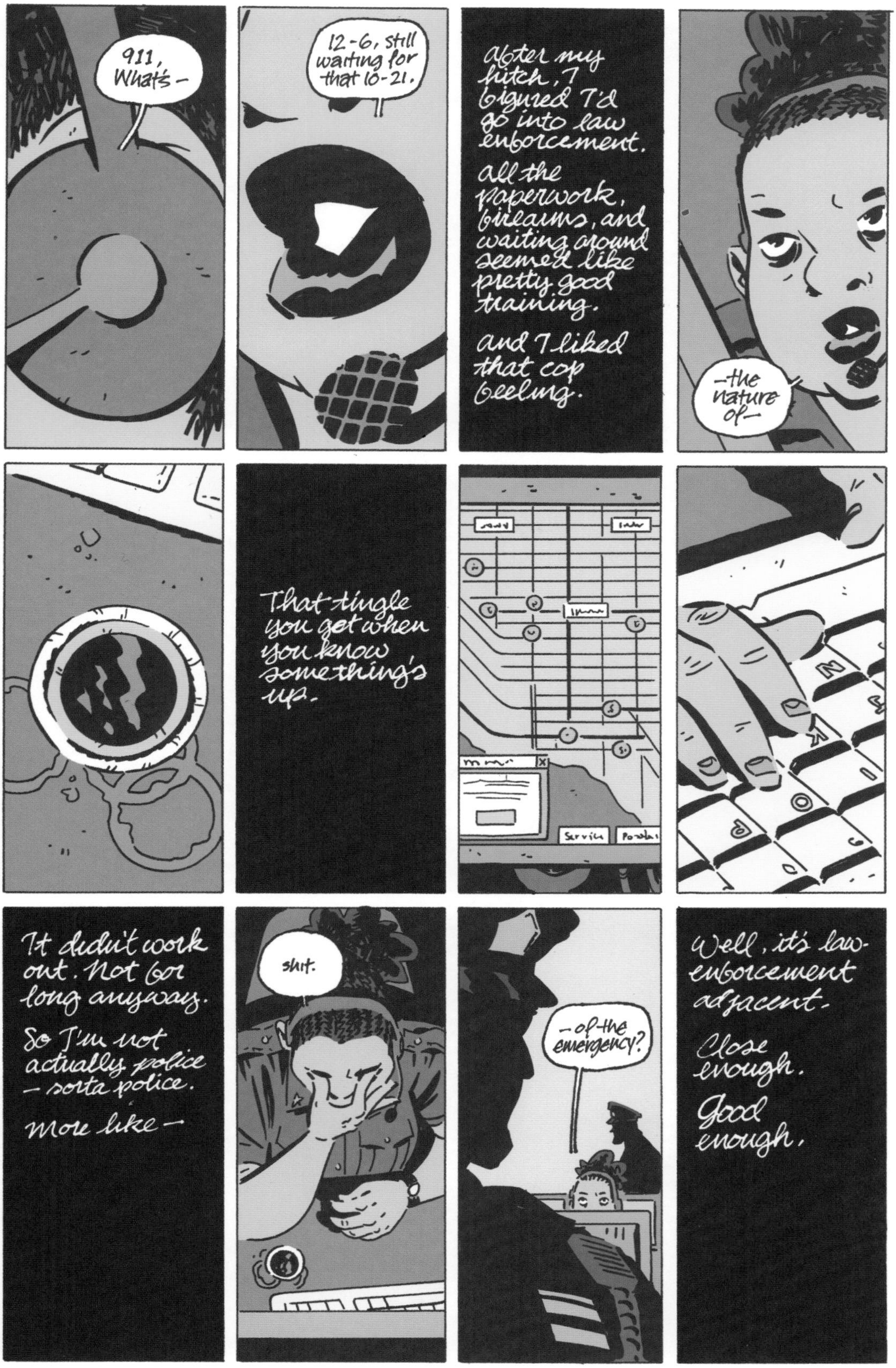
911, What's -
12-6, still waiting for that 10-21.
After my hitch, I figured I'd go into law enforcement.
All the paperwork, firearms, and waiting around seemed like pretty good training.
And I liked that cop feeling.
-the nature of-
That tingle you get when you know something's up.
Service
It didn't work out. Not for long anyway.
So I'm not actually police - sorta police.
More like -
shit.
-of the emergency?
Well, it's law-enforcement adjacent.
Close enough.
Good enough.

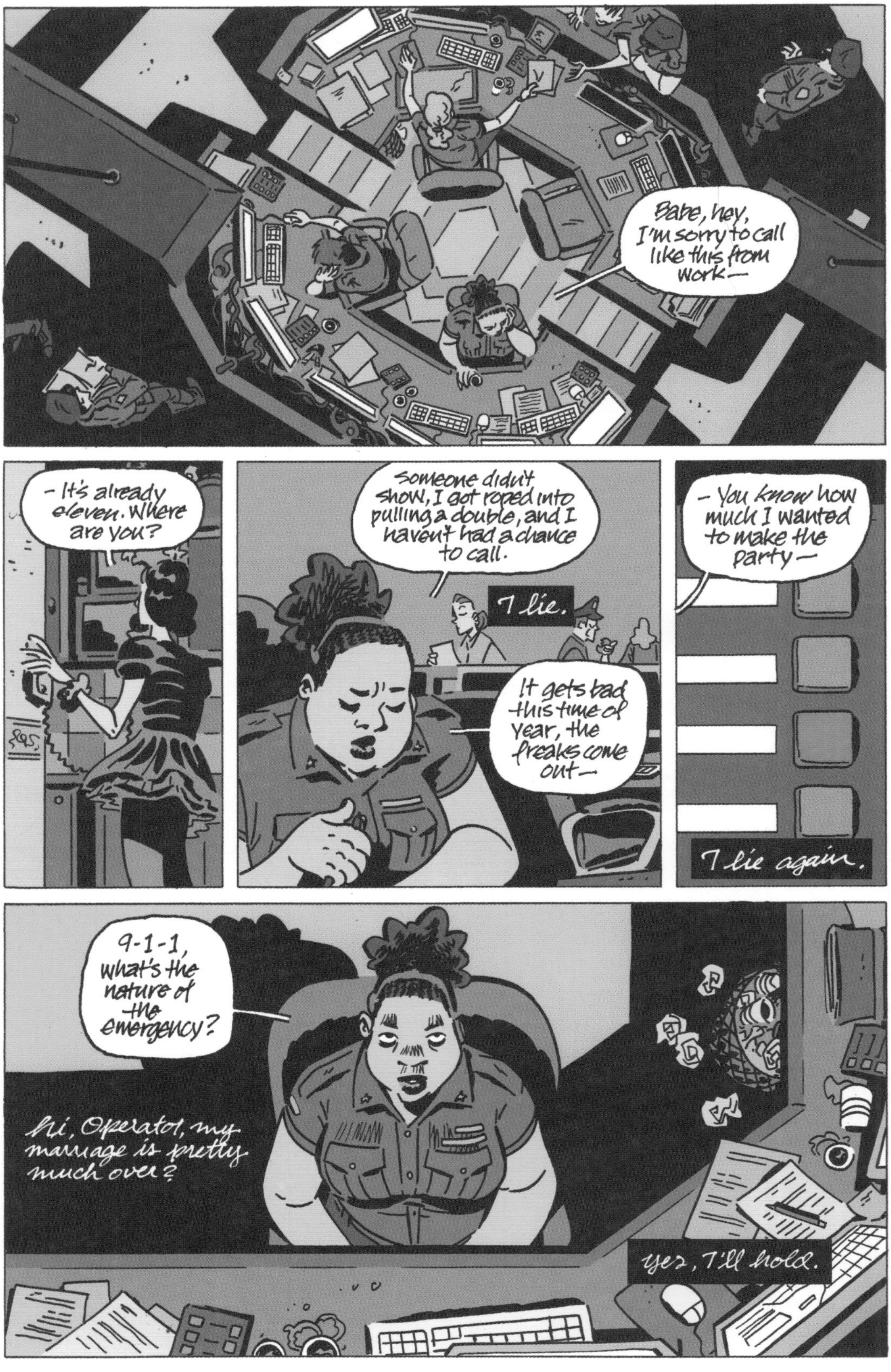
Babe, hey, I'm sorry to call like this from work—
—It's already eleven. Where are you?
Someone didn't show, I got roped into pulling a double, and I haven't had a chance to call.
I lie.
It gets bad this time of year, the freaks come out—
—You know how much I wanted to make the party—
I lie again.
9-1-1, what's the nature of the emergency?
hi, Operator, my marriage is pretty much over?
yes, I'll hold.

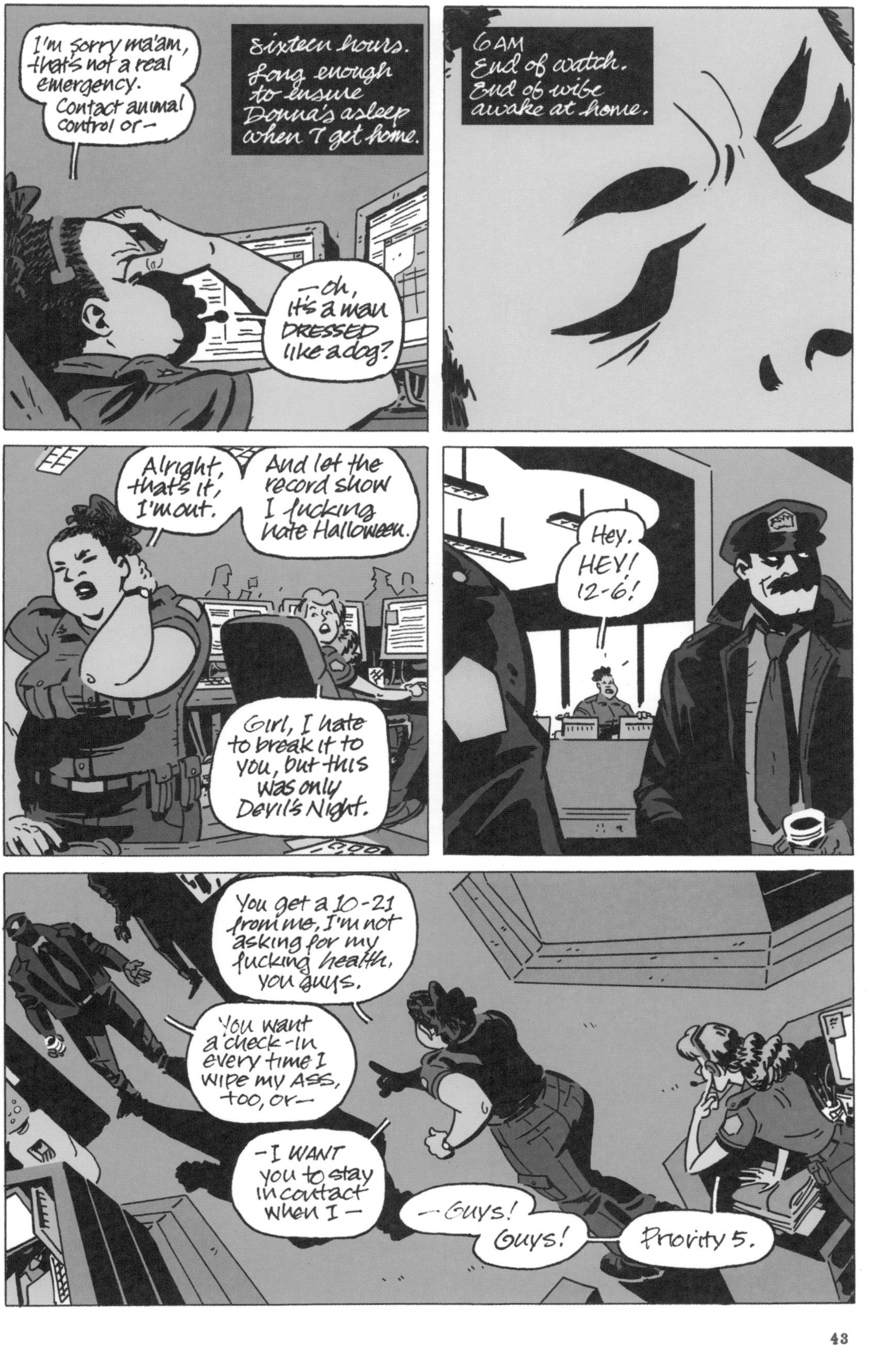
I'm sorry ma'am, that's not a real emergency. Contact animal control or—
Sixteen hours. Long enough to ensure Donna's asleep when I get home.
—oh, it's a man DRESSED like a dog?
6 AM
End of watch. End of wife awake at home.
Alright, that's it, I'm out.
And let the record show I fucking hate Halloween.
Girl, I hate to break it to you, but this was only Devil's Night.
Hey. HEY! 12-6!
You get a 10-21 from me, I'm not asking for my fucking health, you guys.
You want a check-in every time I wipe my ASS, too, or—
—I WANT you to stay in contact when I—
—Guys! Guys!
Priority 5.

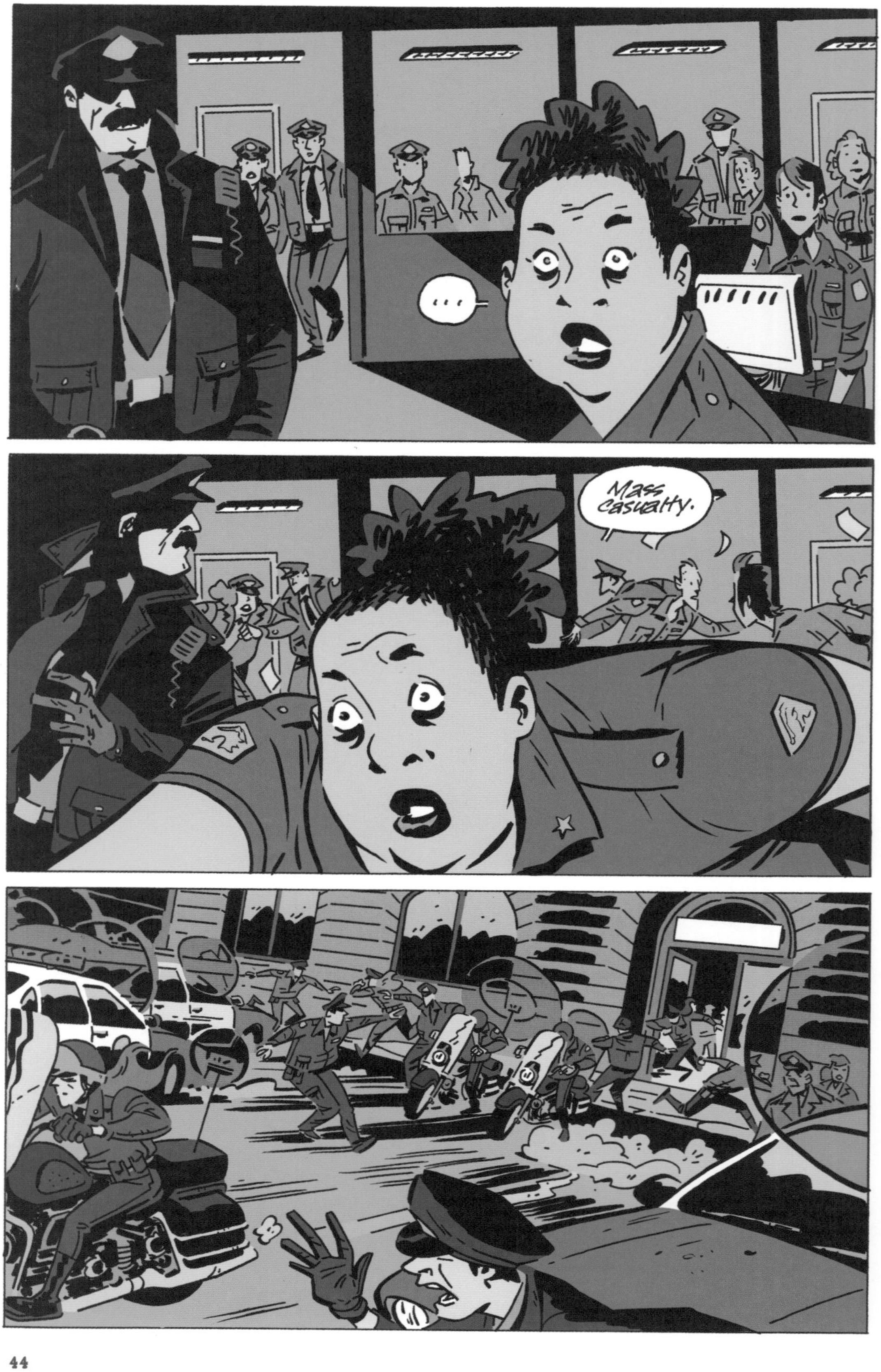
...
Mass casualty.

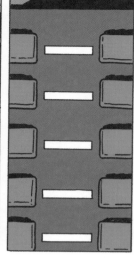

911.

I got cars 2, 5, and 7 en route to—

—wait, scratch 2—

—SHIT—

shit.

whoop sorr—

12-6.
If you're here, who the fuck's in the field driving your car?

You ain't my fucking mother, Kowalski, so get off my fucking ass.

It happened again!
We have MULTIPLE code fives all over the city—

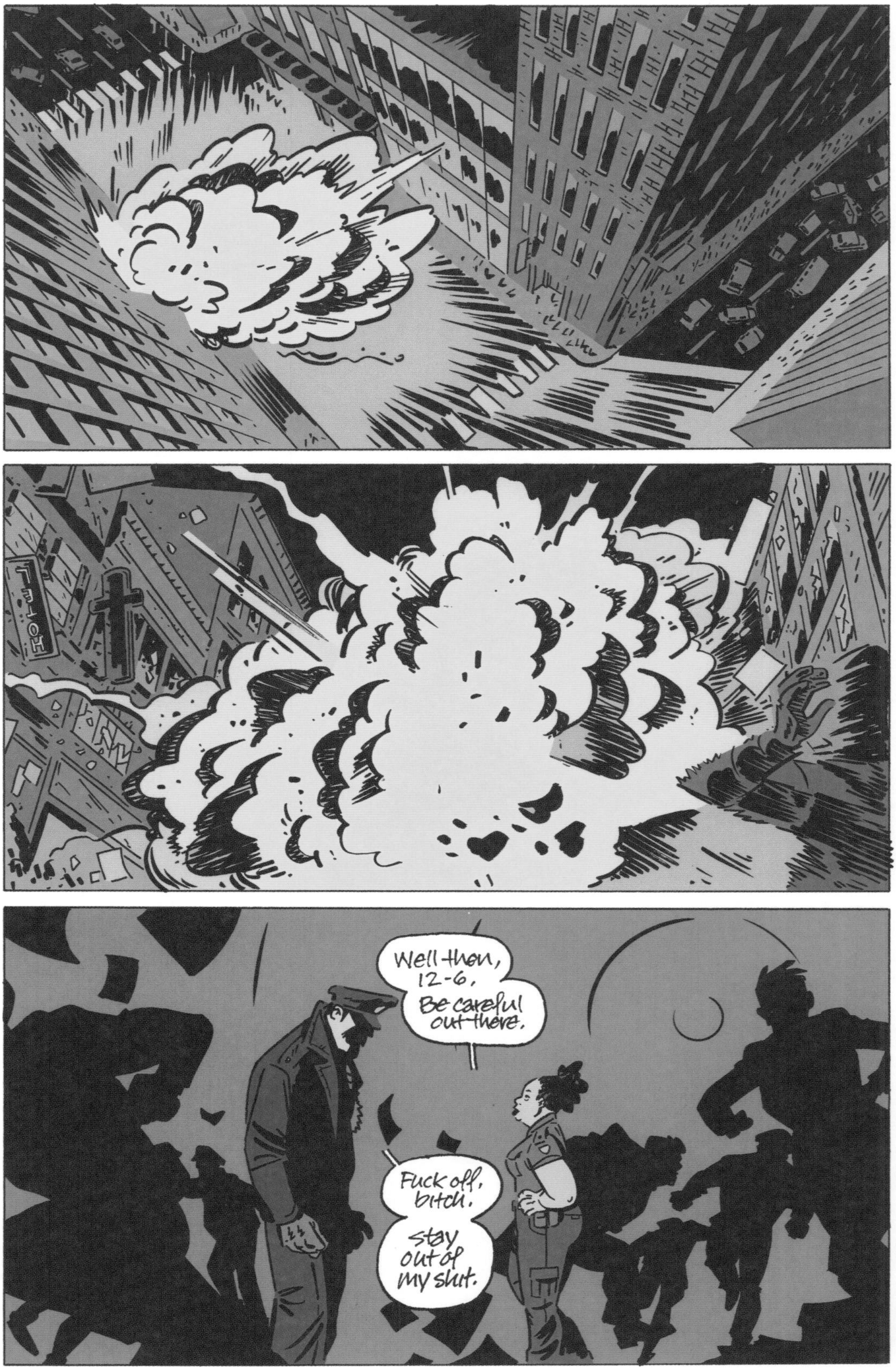
HOTEL
Well then, 12-6. Be careful out there.
Fuck off, bitch.
Stay out of my shit.

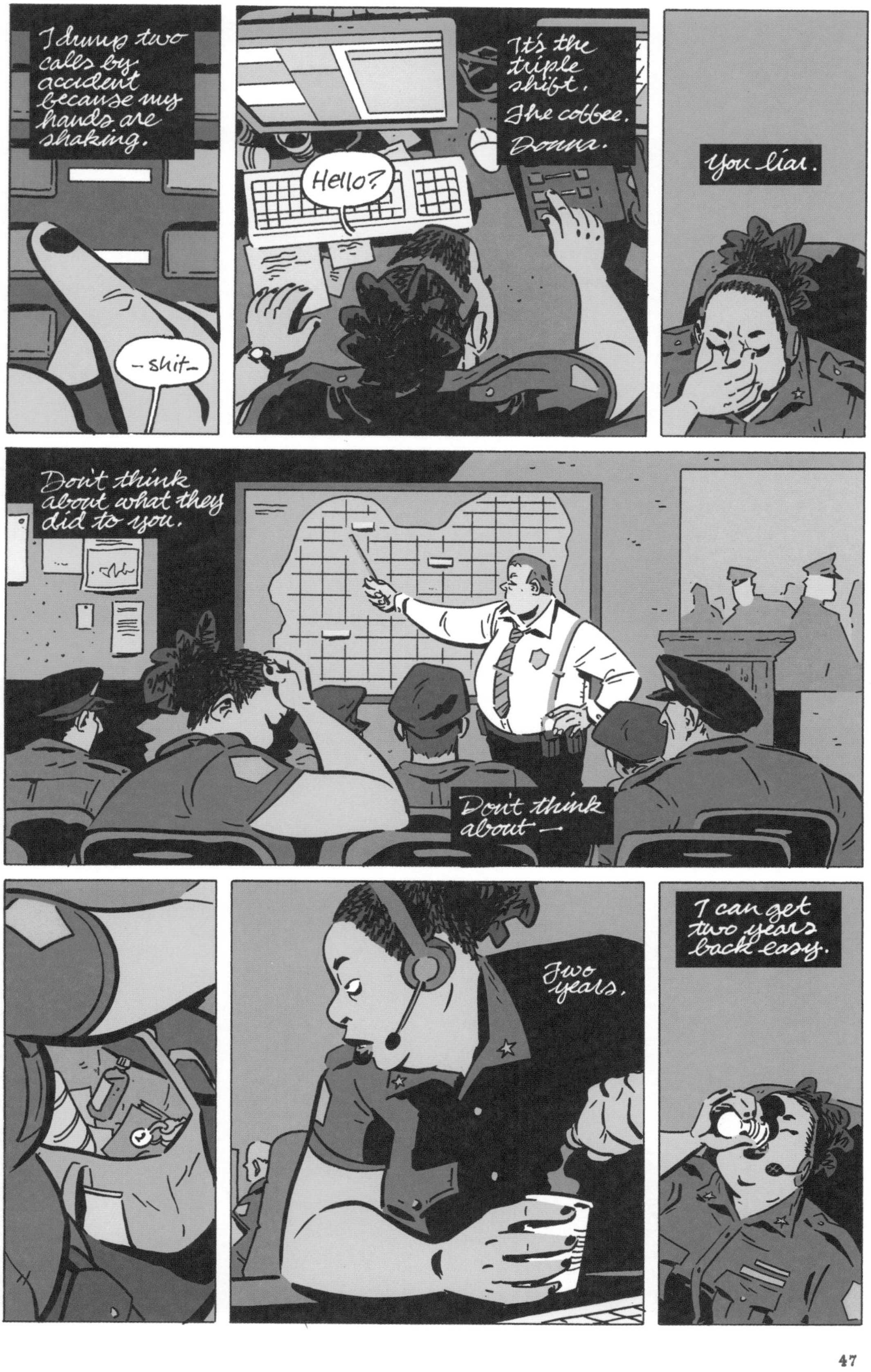
I dump two calls by accident because my hands are shaking.
-shit-
It's the triple shift.
The coffee.
Donna.
Hello?
You liar.
Don't think about what they did to you.
Don't think about—
Two years.
I can get two years back easy.

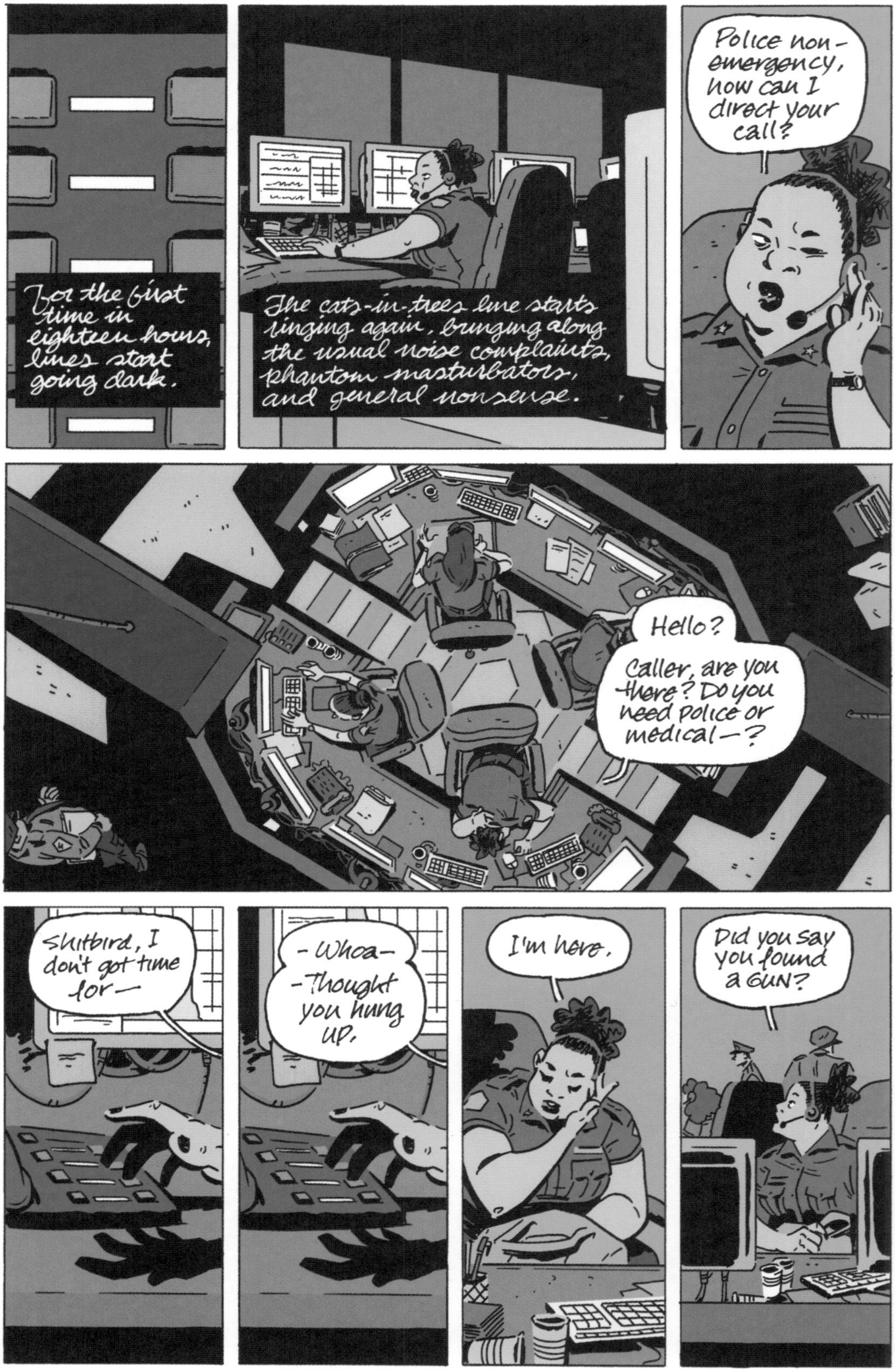
For the first time in eighteen hours, lines start going dark.
The cats-in-trees line starts ringing again, bringing along the usual noise complaints, phantom masturbators, and general nonsense.
Police non-emergency, how can I direct your call?
Hello?
Caller, are you there? Do you need police or medical—?
Shitbird, I don't got time for—
-Whoa-
-Thought you hung up.
I'm here.
Did you say you found a GUN?

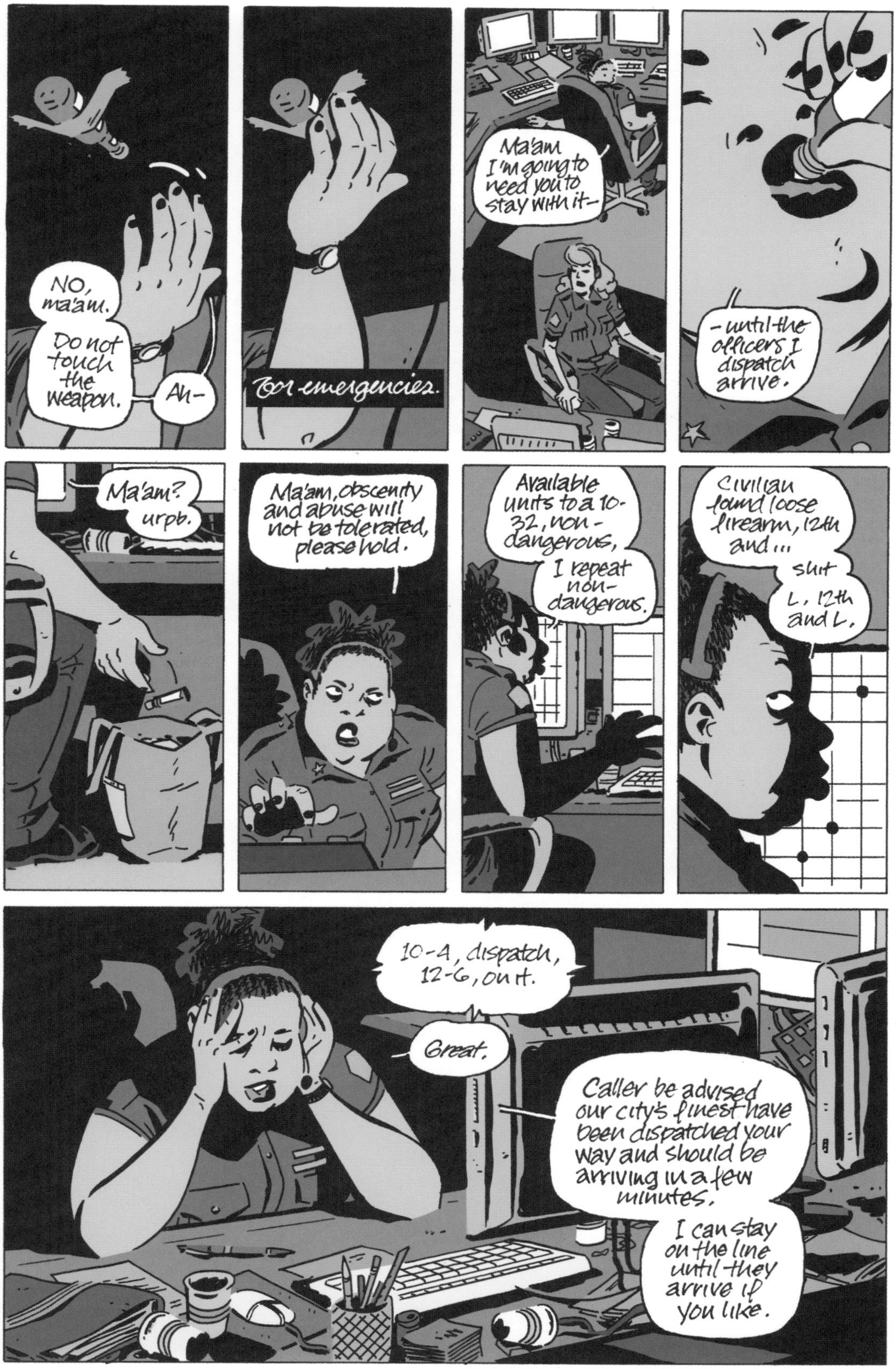
NO, ma'am.
Do not touch the weapon.
Ah-
For emergencies.
Ma'am I'm going to need you to stay with it-
-until the officers I dispatch arrive.
Ma'am? urpb.
Ma'am, obscenity and abuse will not be tolerated, please hold.
Available units to a 10-32, non-dangerous,
I repeat non-dangerous.
Civilian found loose firearm, 12th and...
shit
L, 12th and L.
10-4, dispatch, 12-6, on it.
Great.
Caller be advised our city's finest have been dispatched your way and should be arriving in a few minutes.
I can stay on the line until they arrive if you like.

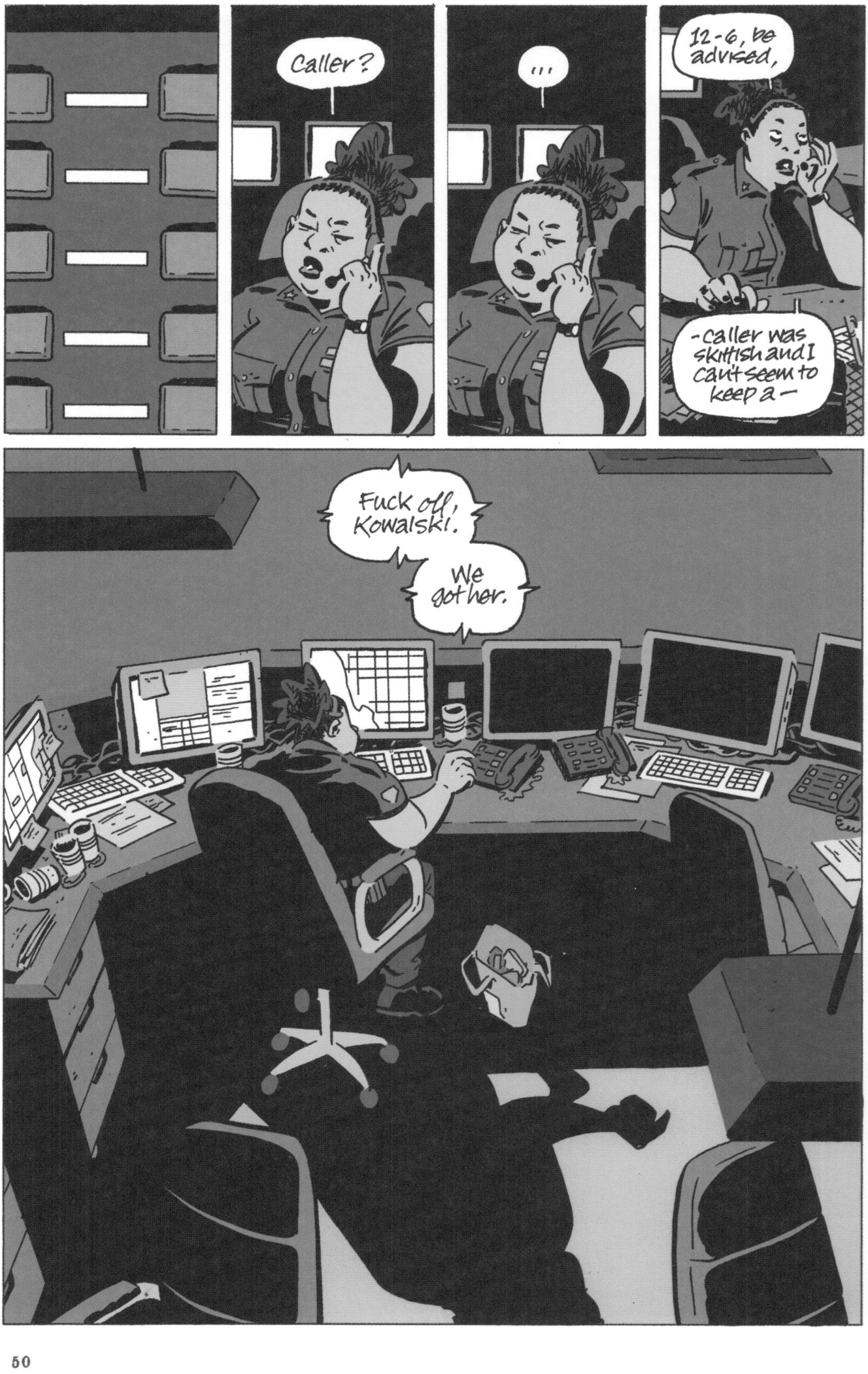
Caller?
...
12-6, be advised,
-caller was skittish and I can't seem to keep a-
Fuck off, Kowalski.
We got her.

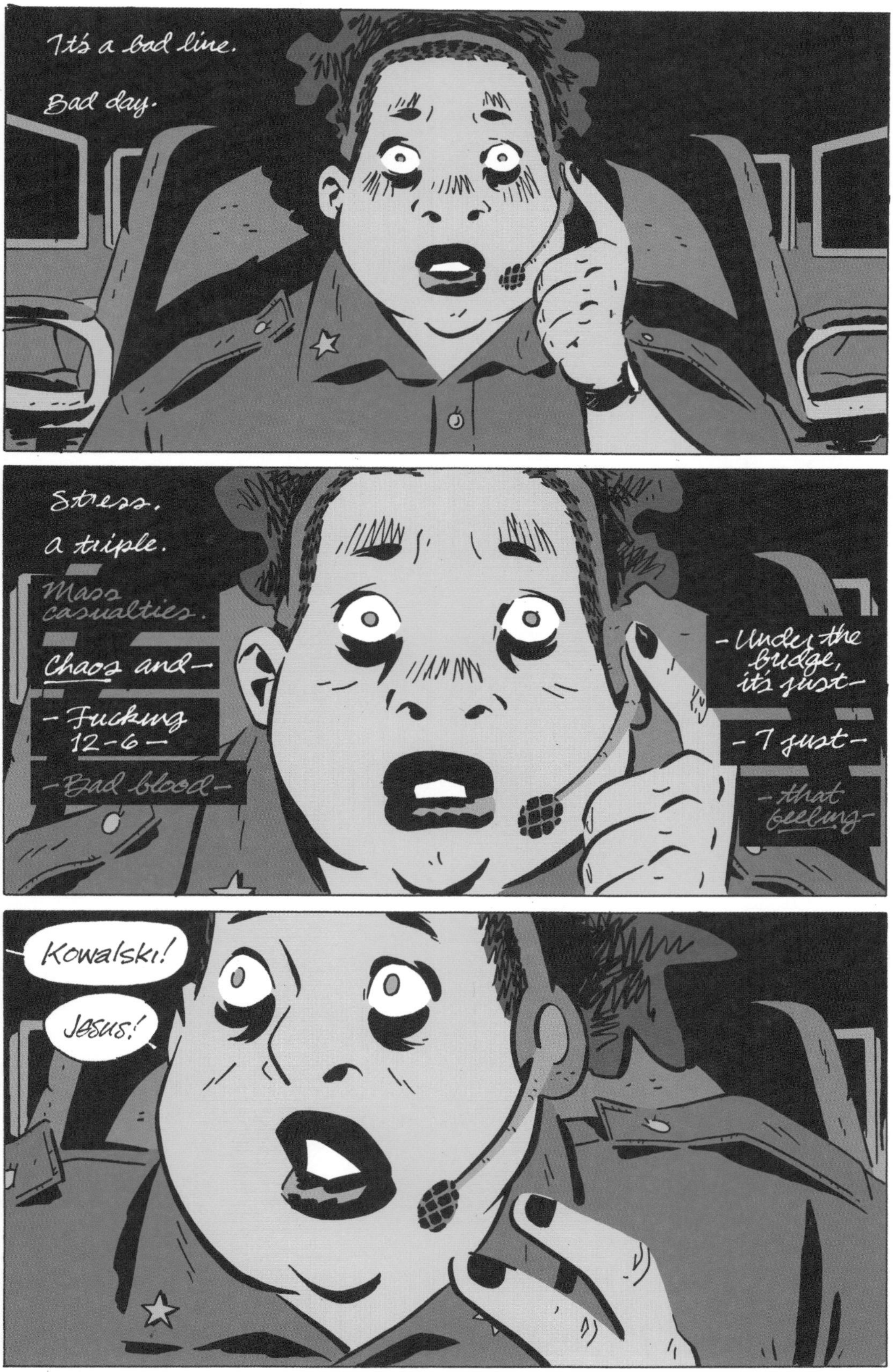
It's a bad line.
Bad day.
Stress.
a triple.
Mass casualties.
Chaos and—
- Fucking 12-6 —
-Bad blood-
-Under the bridge, it's just-
- I just-
-that feeling-
Kowalski!
Jesus!

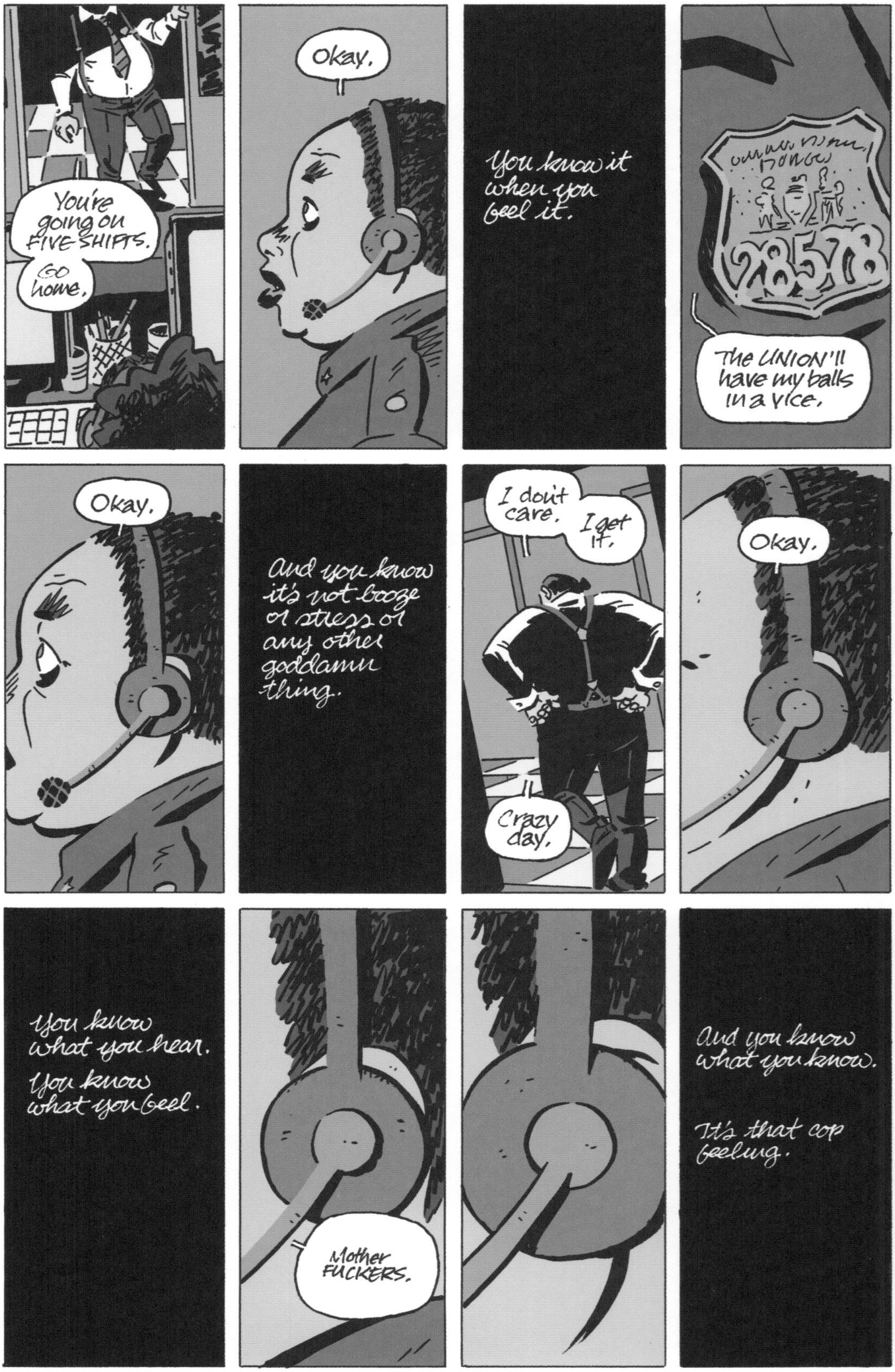
You're going on FIVE SHIFTS.
Go home.
Okay.
You know it when you feel it.
The UNION'll have my balls in a vice.
Okay.
And you know it's not booze or stress or any other goddamn thing.
I don't care.
I get it.
Crazy day.
Okay.
You know what you hear.
You know what you feel.
Mother FUCKERS.
And you know what you know.
It's that cop feeling.

THE THIEF

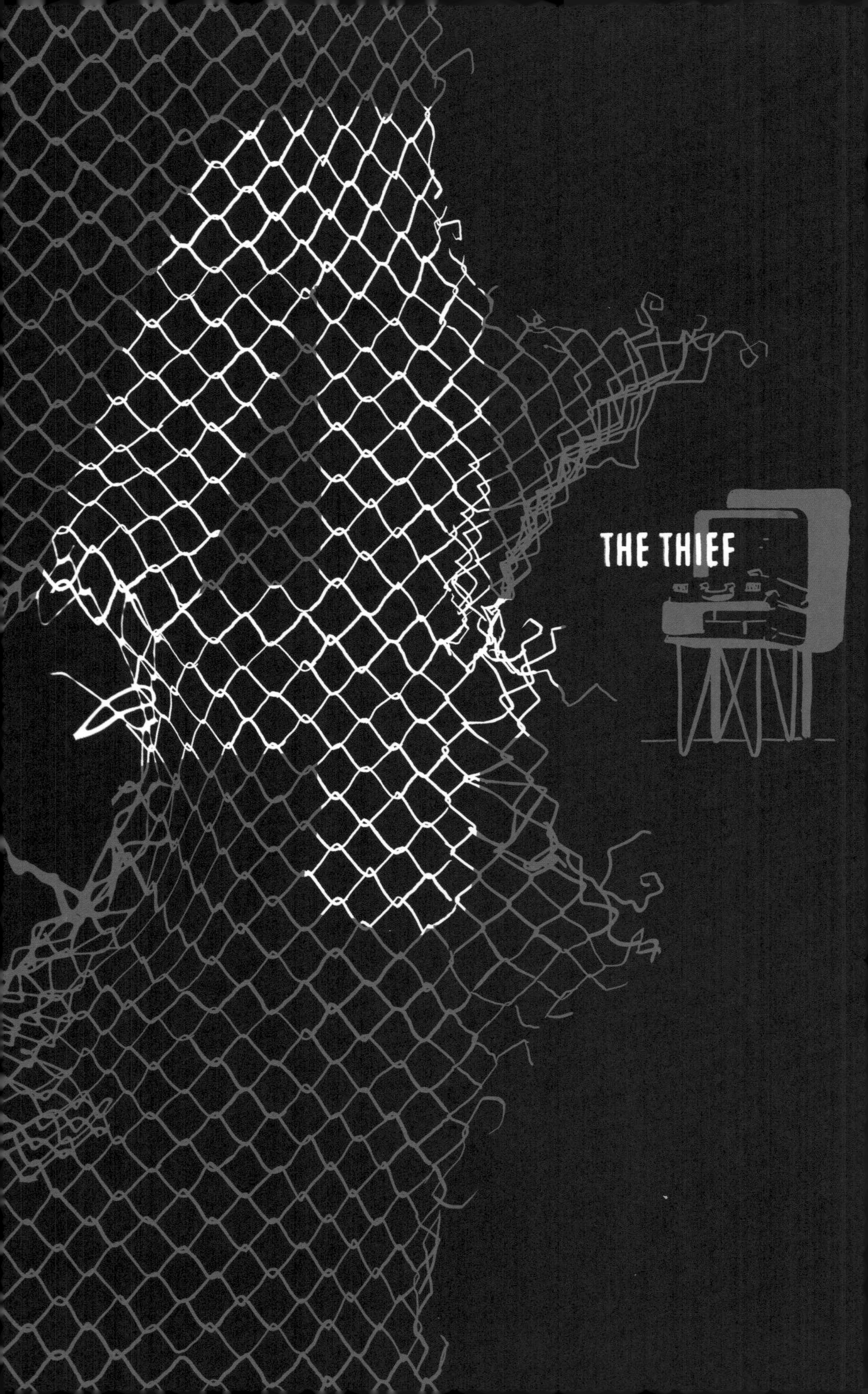

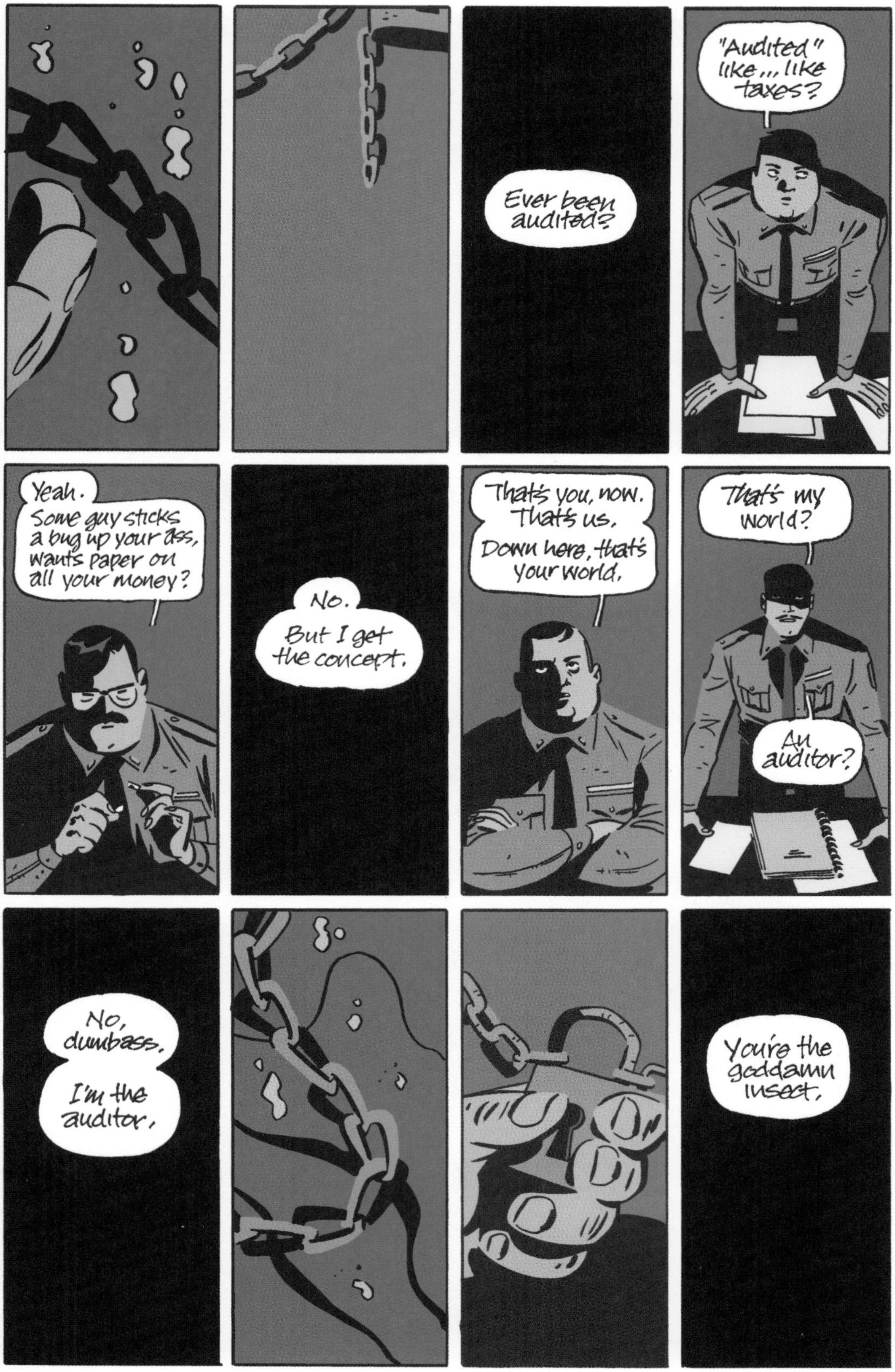
Ever been audited?
"Audited" like... like taxes?
Yeah. Some guy sticks a bug up your ass, wants paper on all your money?
No. But I get the concept.
That's you, now. That's us. Down here, that's your world.
That's my world?
An auditor?
No, dumbass. I'm the auditor.
You're the goddamn insect.

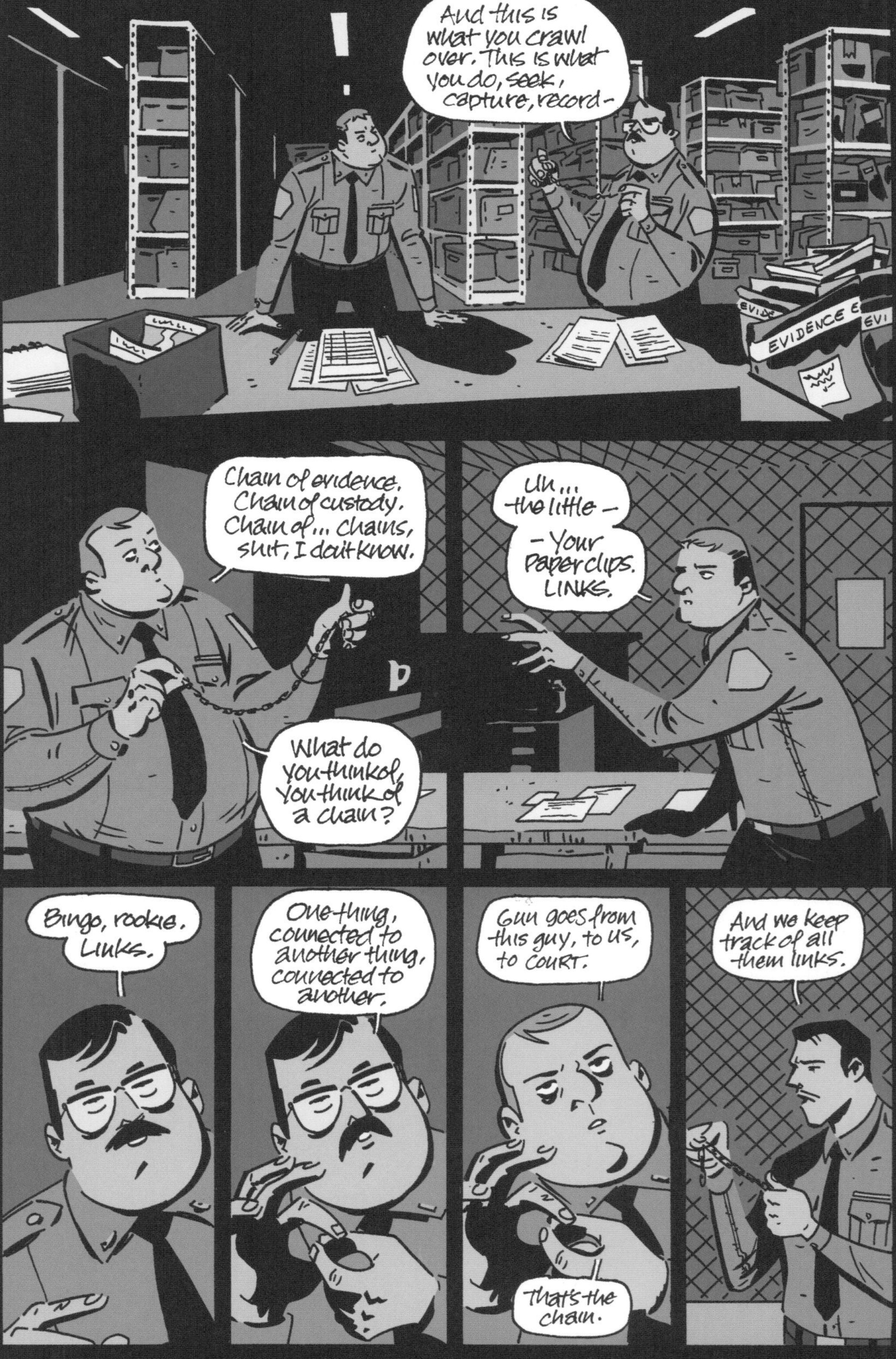
And this is what you crawl over. This is what you do, seek, capture, record-
Chain of evidence. Chain of custody. Chain of... chains, shit, I don't know.
What do you think of, you think of a chain?
Uh... the little -
-Your paper clips. LINKS.
Bingo, rookie. Links.
One thing, connected to another thing, connected to another.
Gun goes from this guy, to us, to court.
That's the chain.
And we keep track of all them links.

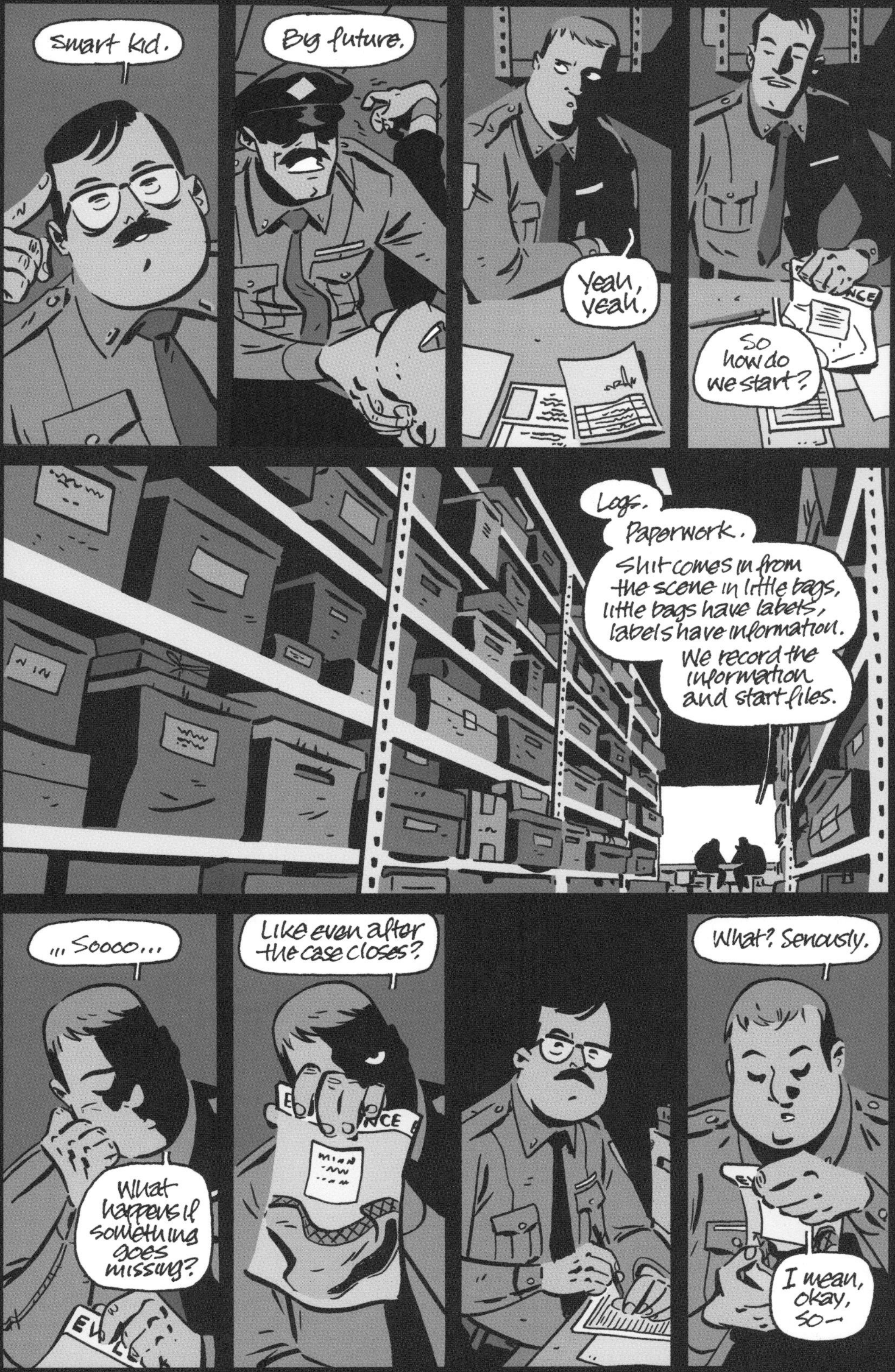
Smart kid.
Big future.
Yeah, yeah.
So how do we start?
Logs.
Paperwork.
Shit comes in from the scene in little bags, little bags have labels, labels have information.
We record the information and start files.
...Soooo...
What happens if something goes missing?
Like even after the case closes?
What? Seriously.
I mean, okay, so—

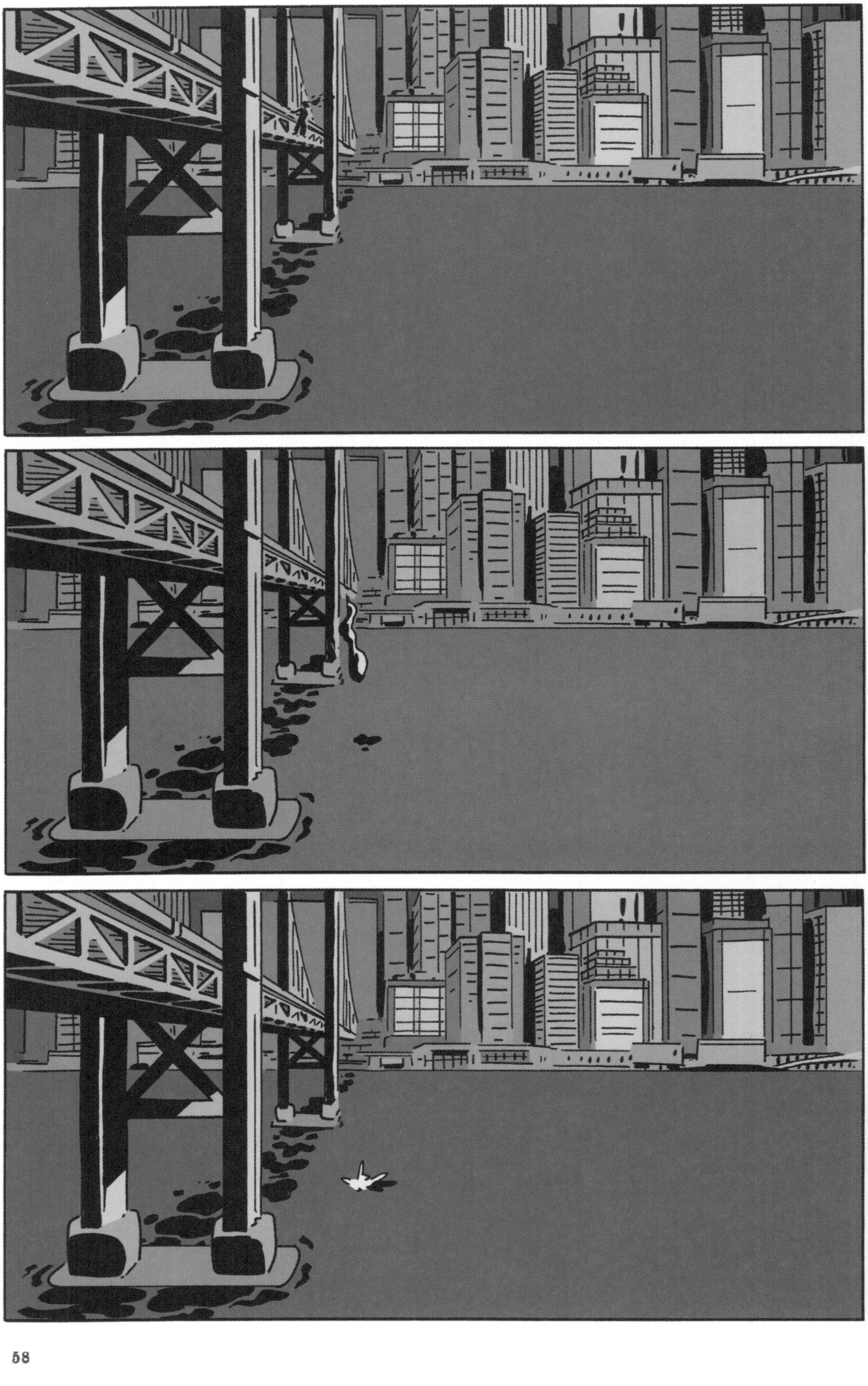

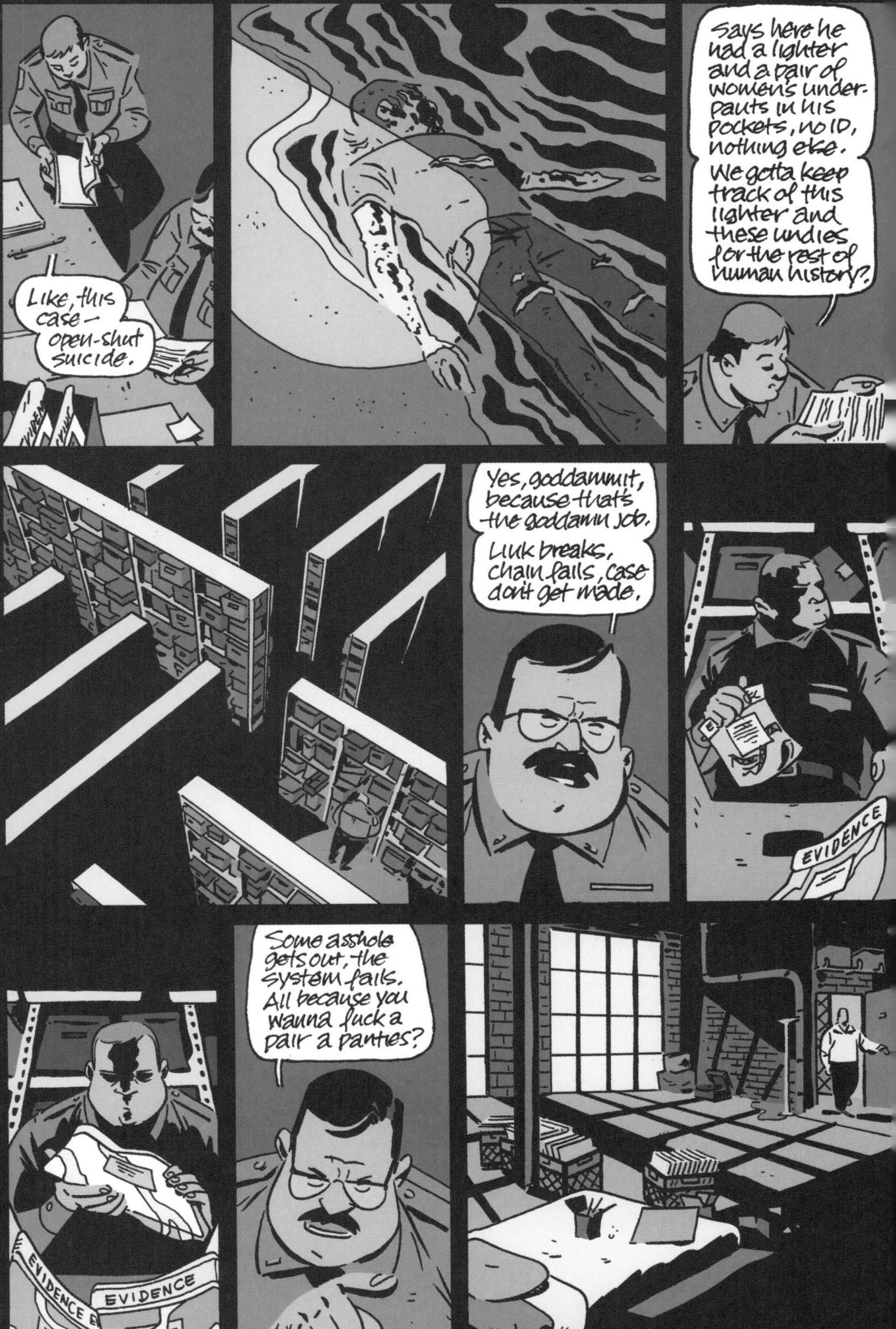
Like, this case— open-shut suicide.
Says here he had a lighter and a pair of women's under-pants in his pockets, no ID, nothing else.
We gotta keep track of this lighter and these undies for the rest of human history?
Yes, goddammit, because that's the goddamn job.
Link breaks, chain fails, case don't get made.
EVIDENCE
EVIDENCE
EVIDENCE
Some asshole gets out, the system fails. All because you wanna fuck a pair a panties?

Sarah Vaugh

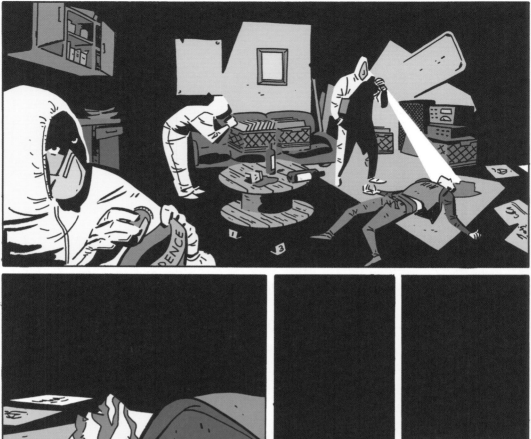

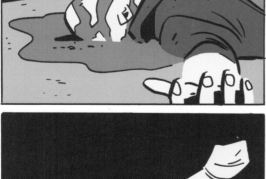

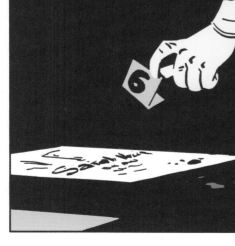

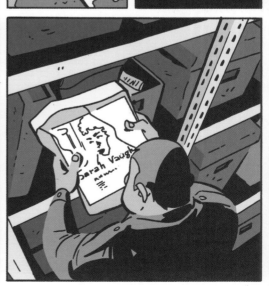

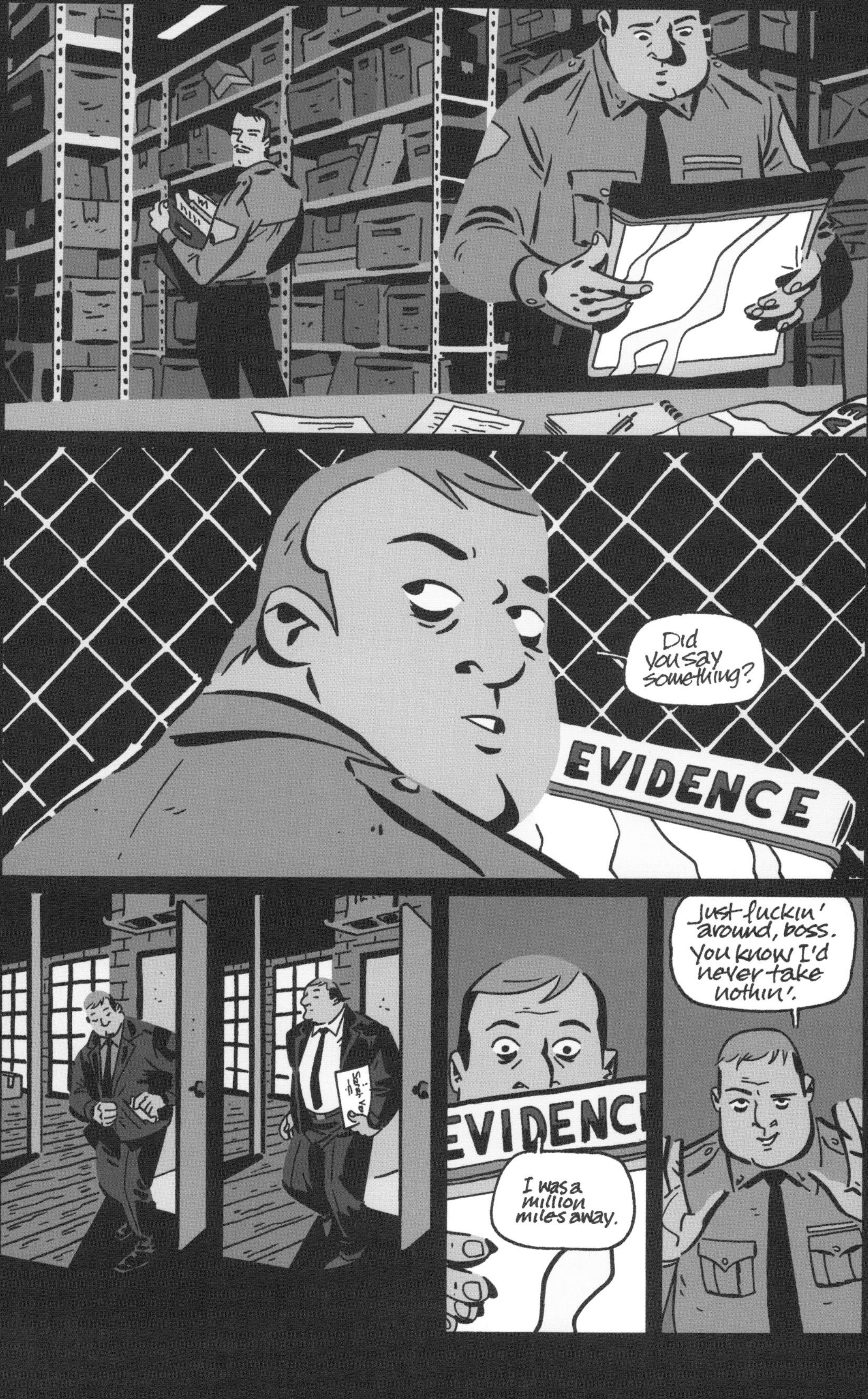
EVIDENCE
Did you say something?
EVIDENCE
I was a million miles away.
Just fuckin' around, boss. You know I'd never take nothin'.

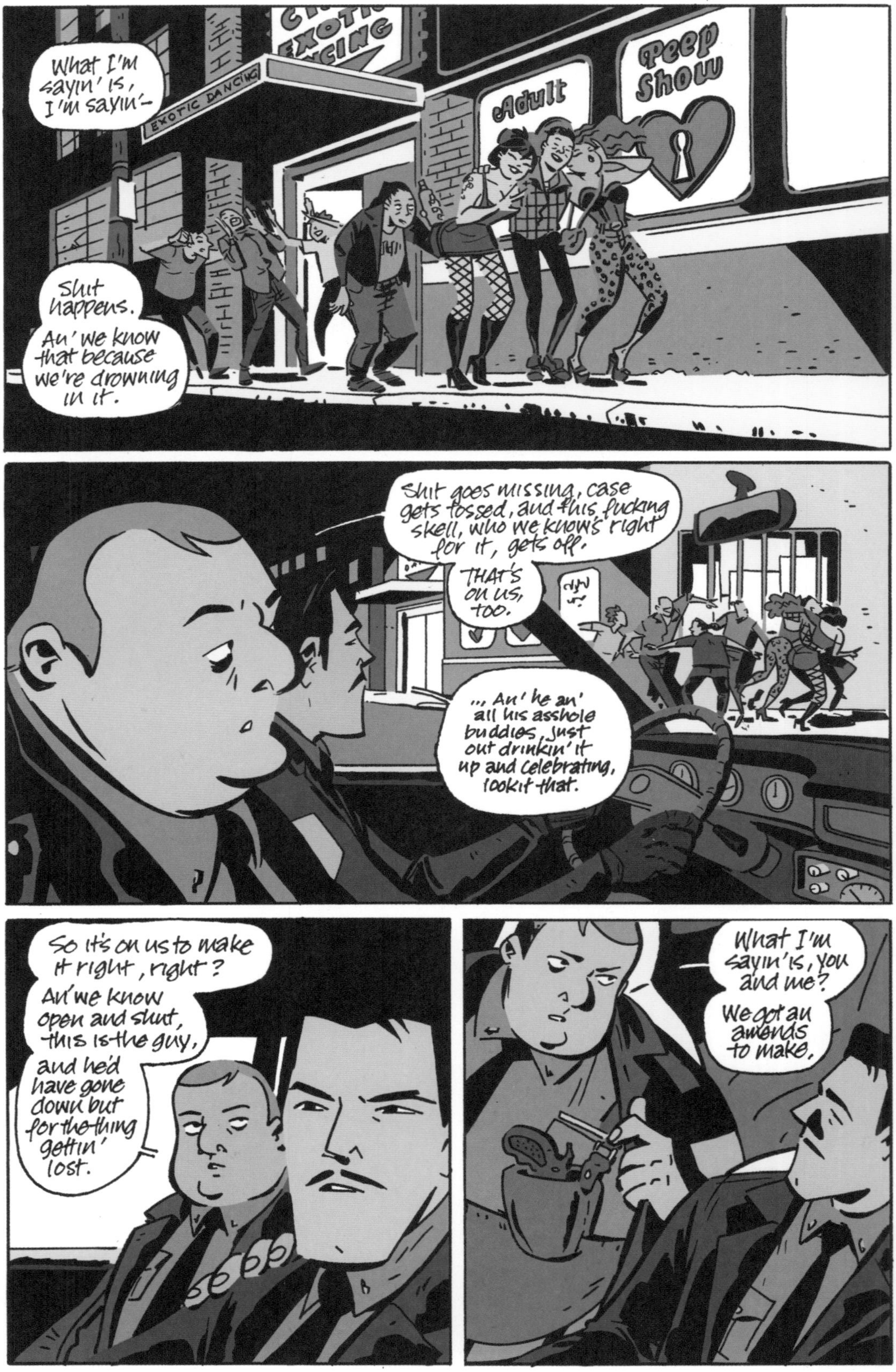
CI… EXOTIC …NCING
EXOTIC DANCING
Adult
Peep Show
What I'm sayin' is, I'm sayin'-
Shit happens.
An' we know that because we're drowning in it.
Shit goes missing, case gets tossed, and this fucking skell, who we know's right for it, gets off.
THAT'S on us, too.
..., An' he an' all his asshole buddies, just out drinkin' it up and celebrating, lookit that.
So it's on us to make it right, right?
An' we know open and shut, this is the guy,
and he'd have gone down but for the thing gettin' lost.
What I'm sayin' is, you and me?
We got an amends to make.

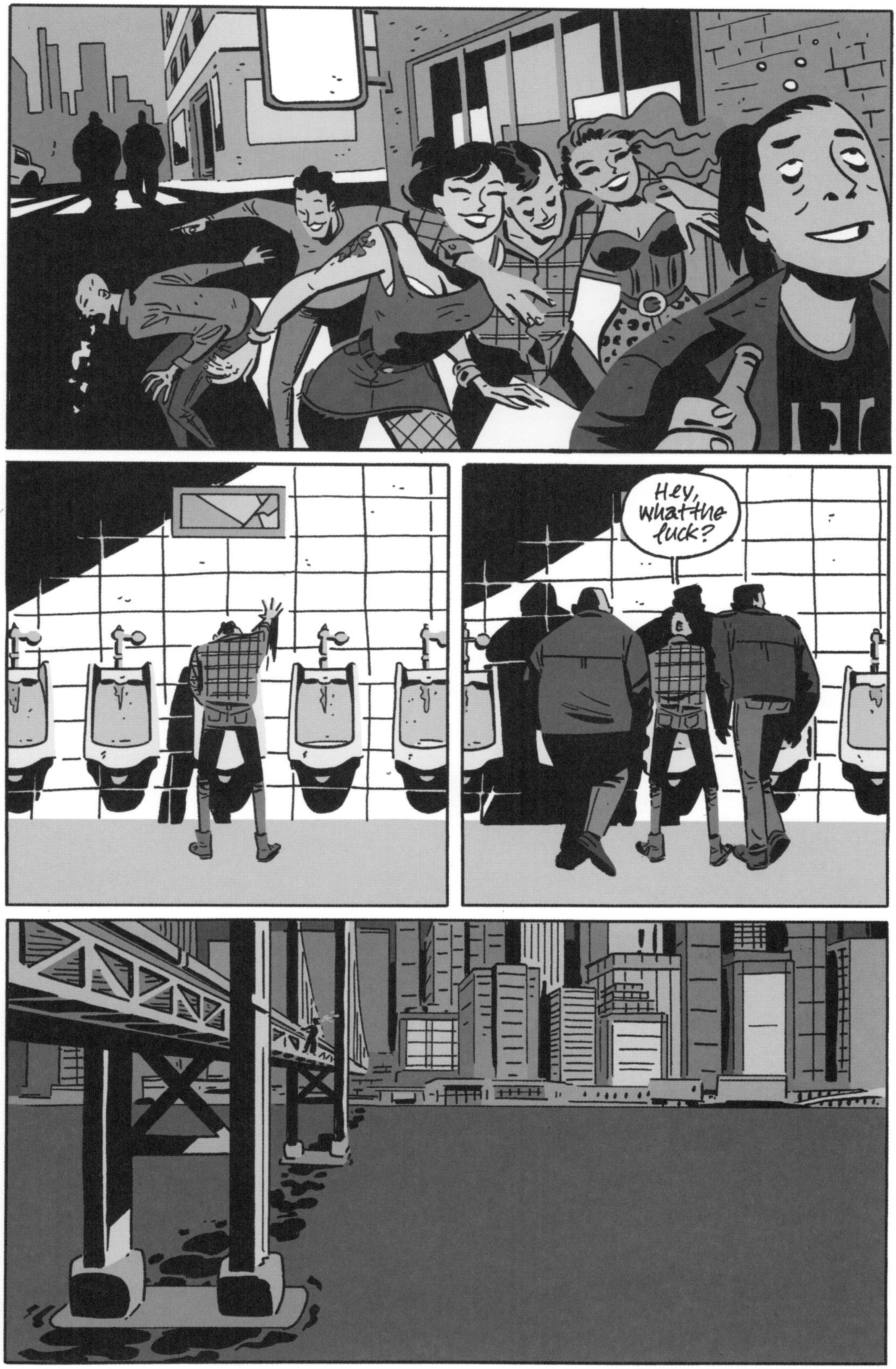
Hey, what the fuck?

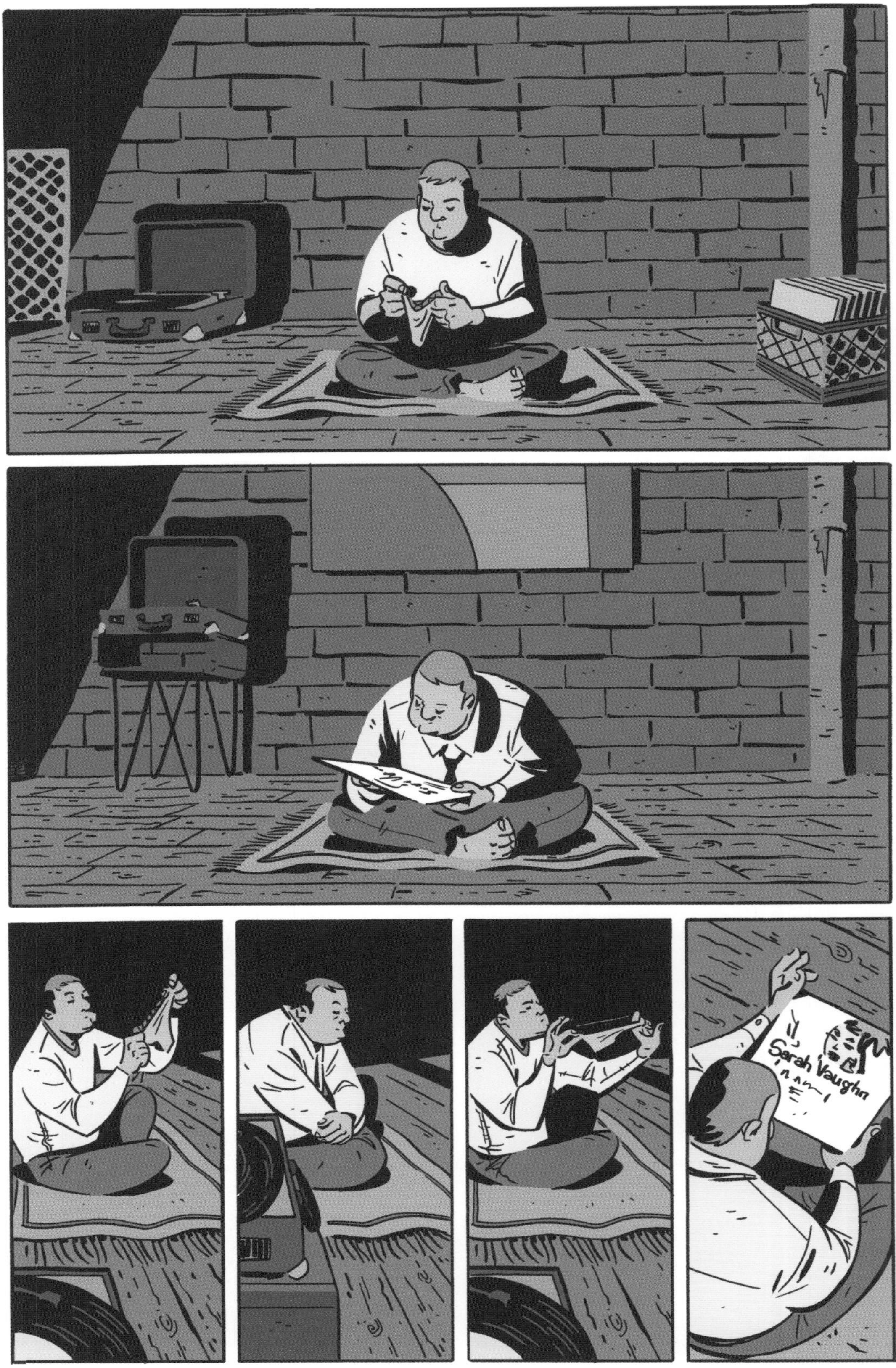
Sarah Vaughn

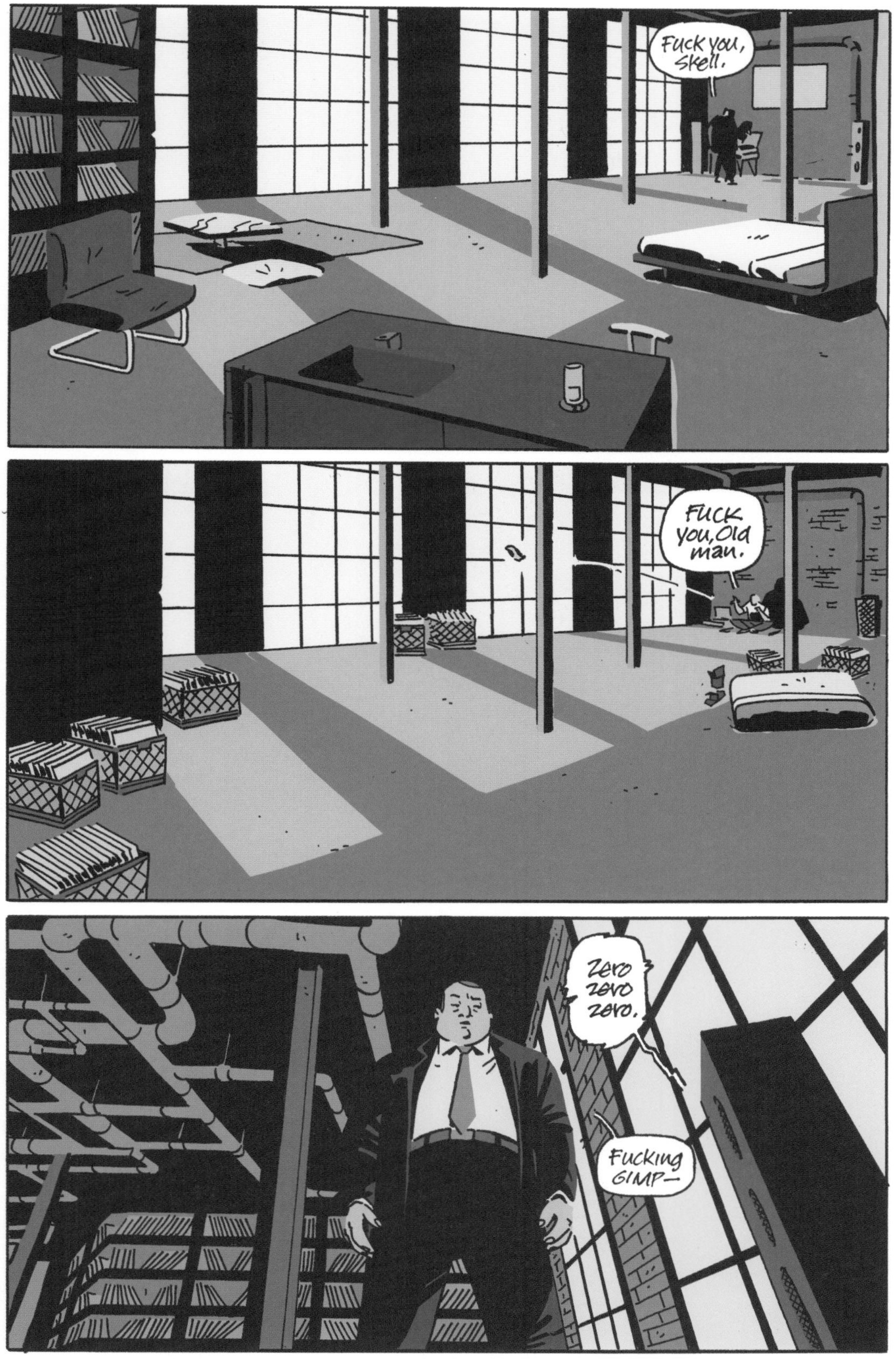
Fuck you, Skell.
Fuck you, Old man.
Zero zero zero.
Fucking GIMP—

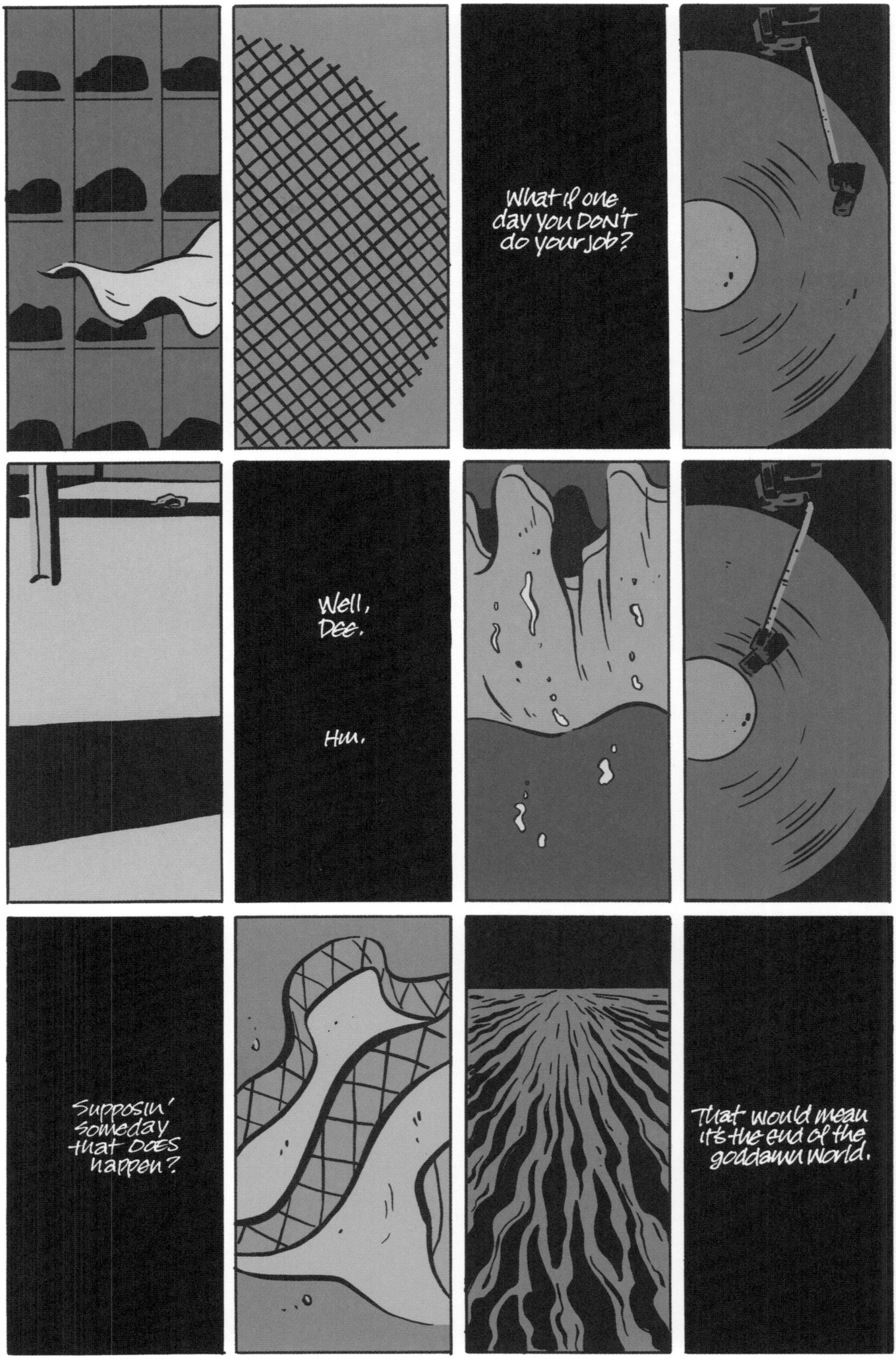
What if one
day you DON'T
do your job?
Well,
Dee.
Hm.
Supposin'
someday
that DOES
happen?
That would mean
it's the end of the
goddamn world.

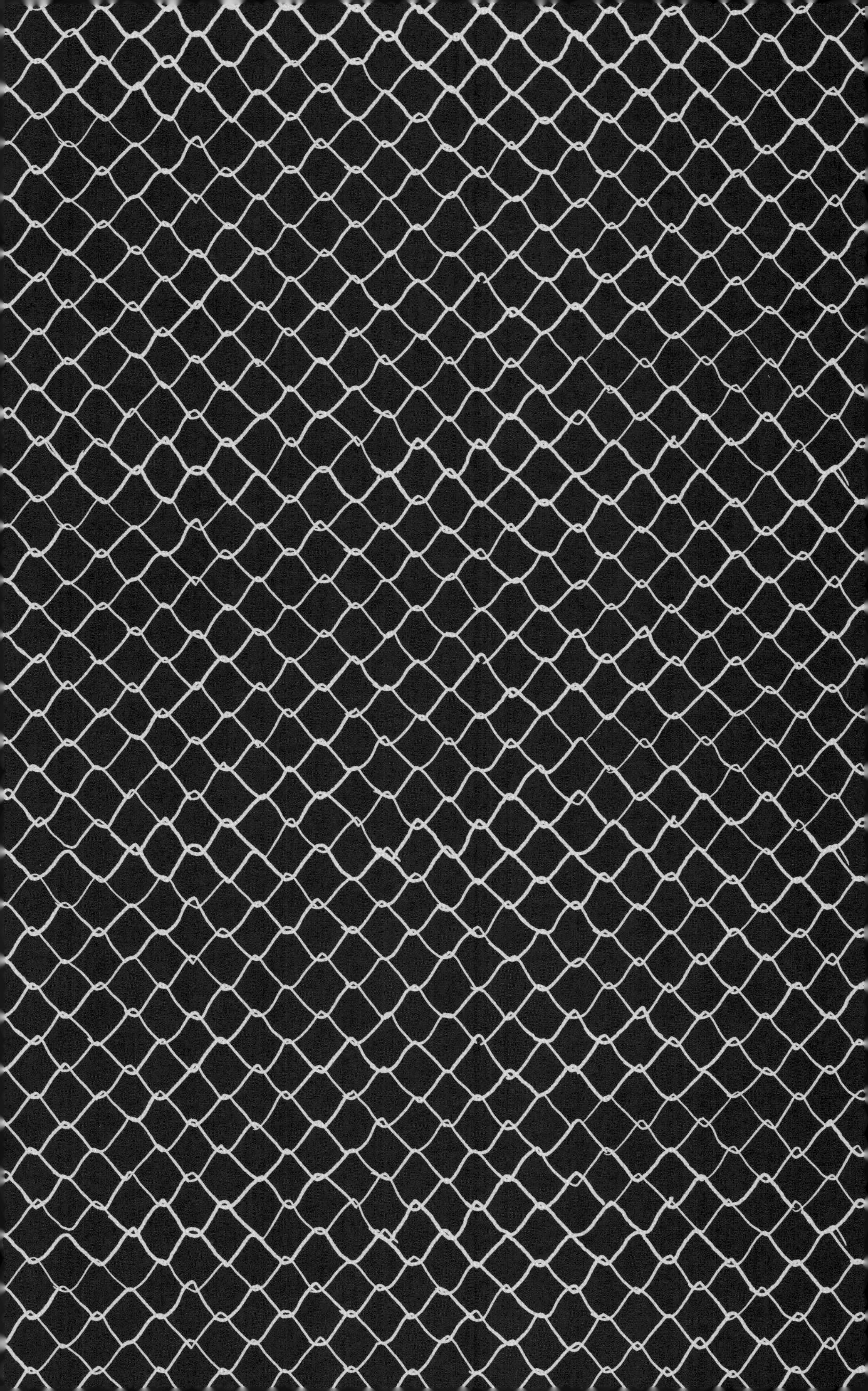

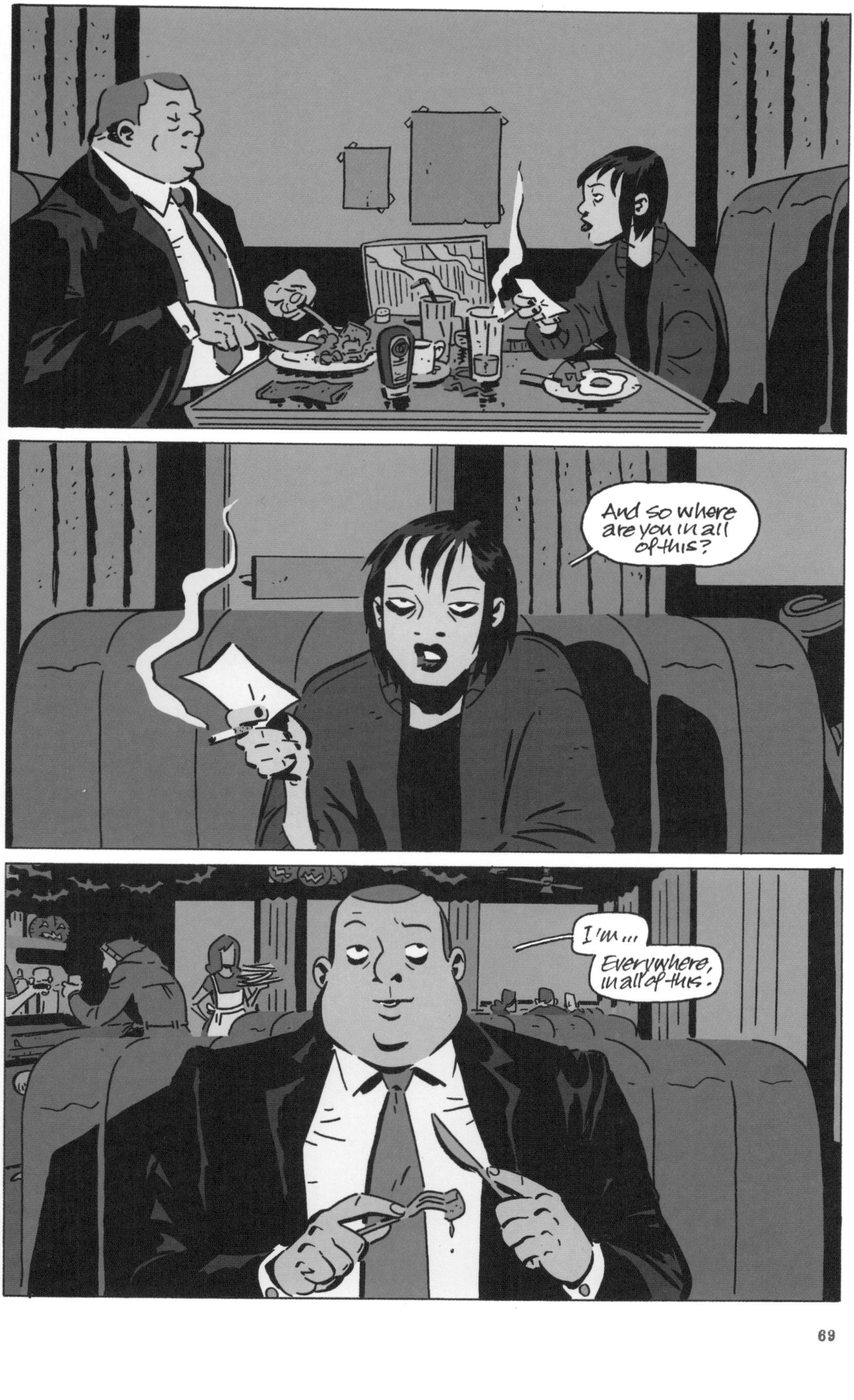
And so where are you in all of this?
I'm... Everywhere, in all of this.

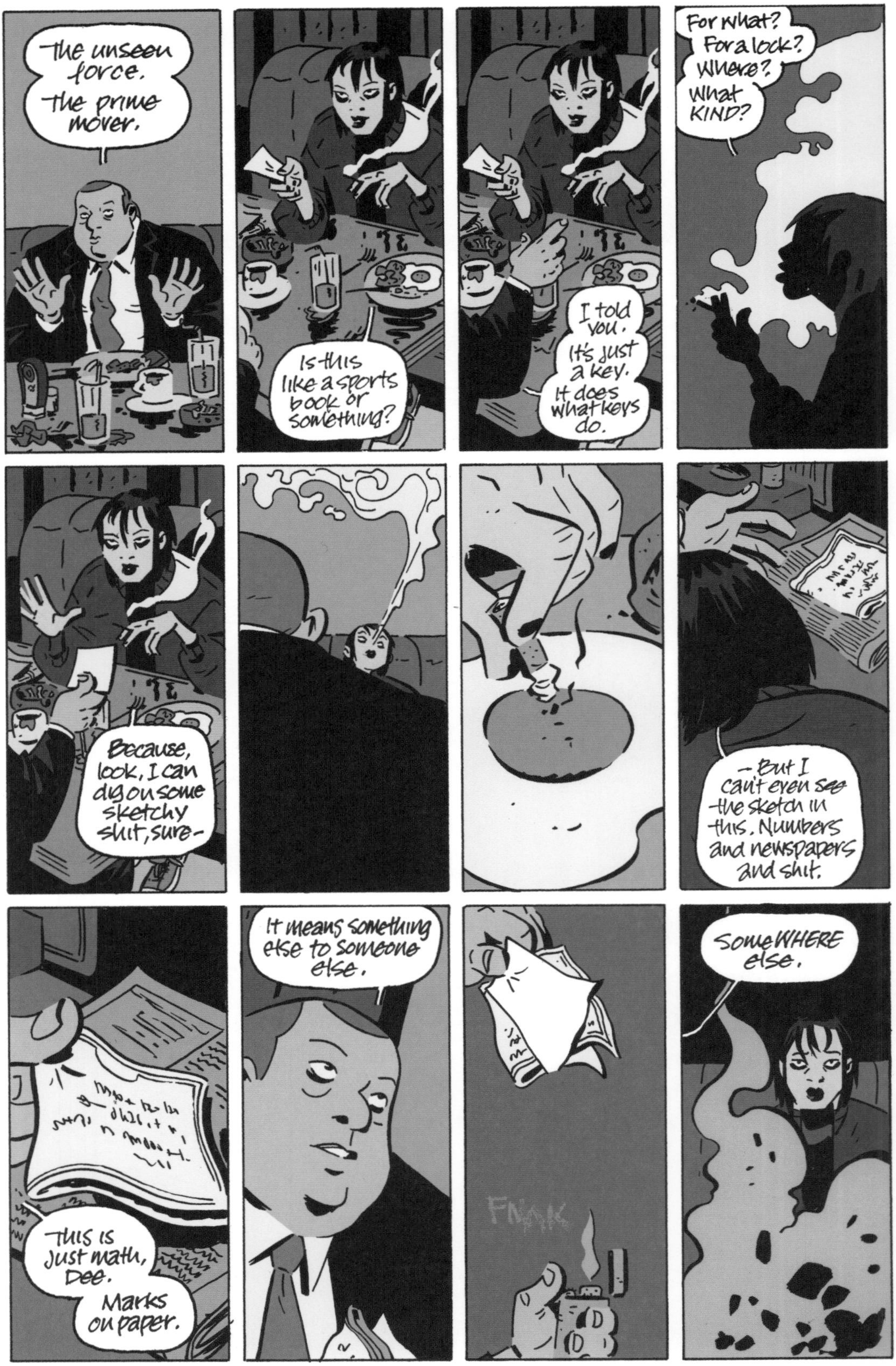
The unseen force. The prime mover.
Is this like a sports book or something?
I told you. It's just a key. It does what keys do.
For what? For a lock? Where? What KIND?
Because, look, I can dig on some sketchy shit, sure-
—But I can't even see the sketch in this. Numbers and newspapers and shit.
This is just math, Dee.
Marks on paper.
It means something else to someone else.
FNAK
SomeWHERE else.

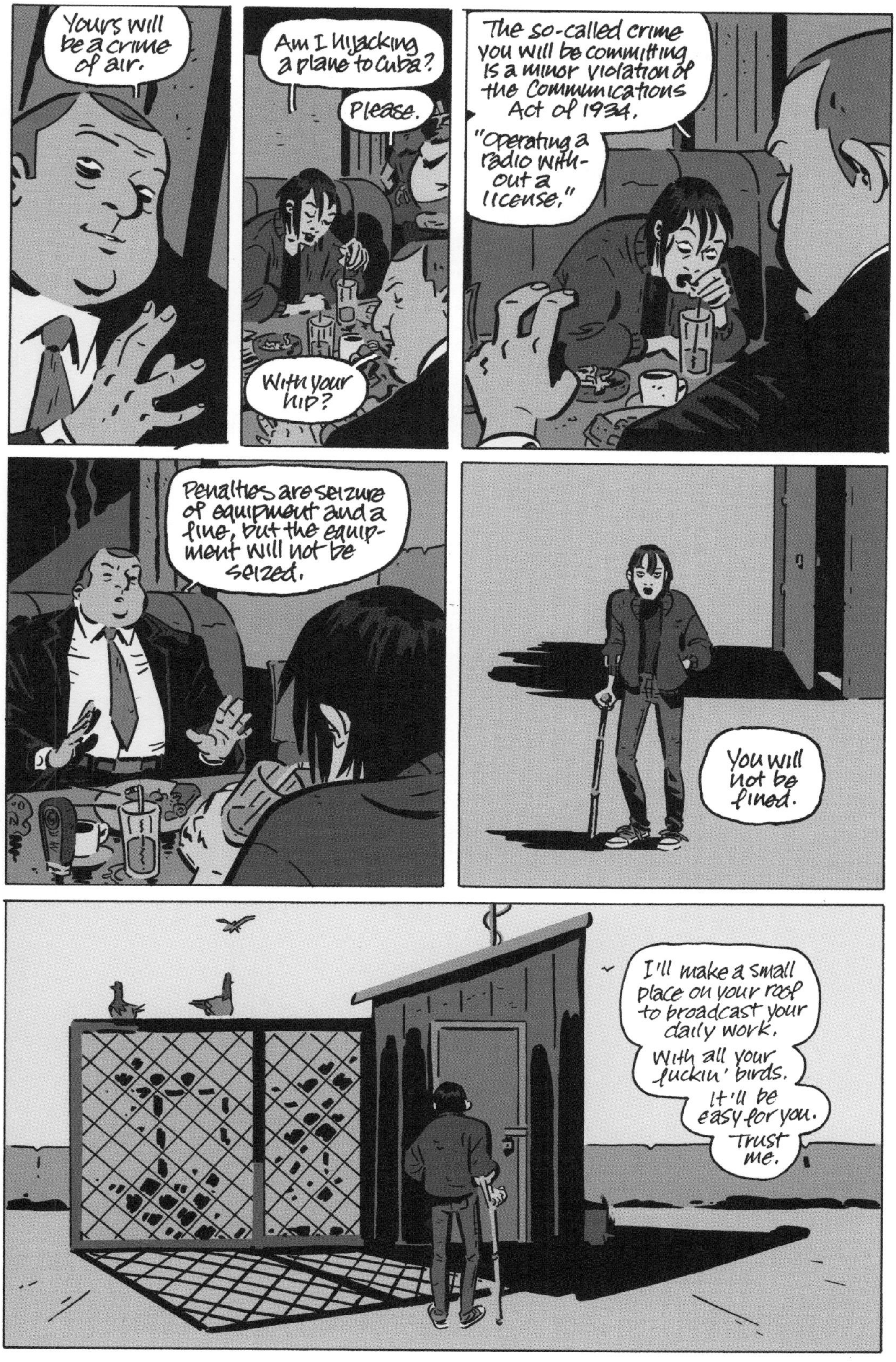
Yours will be a crime of air.
Am I hijacking a plane to Cuba?
Please.
With your hip?
The so-called crime you will be committing is a minor violation of the Communications Act of 1934.
"Operating a radio without a license."
Penalties are seizure of equipment and a fine, but the equipment will not be seized.
You will not be fined.
I'll make a small place on your roof to broadcast your daily work.
With all your fuckin' birds.
It'll be easy for you.
Trust me.

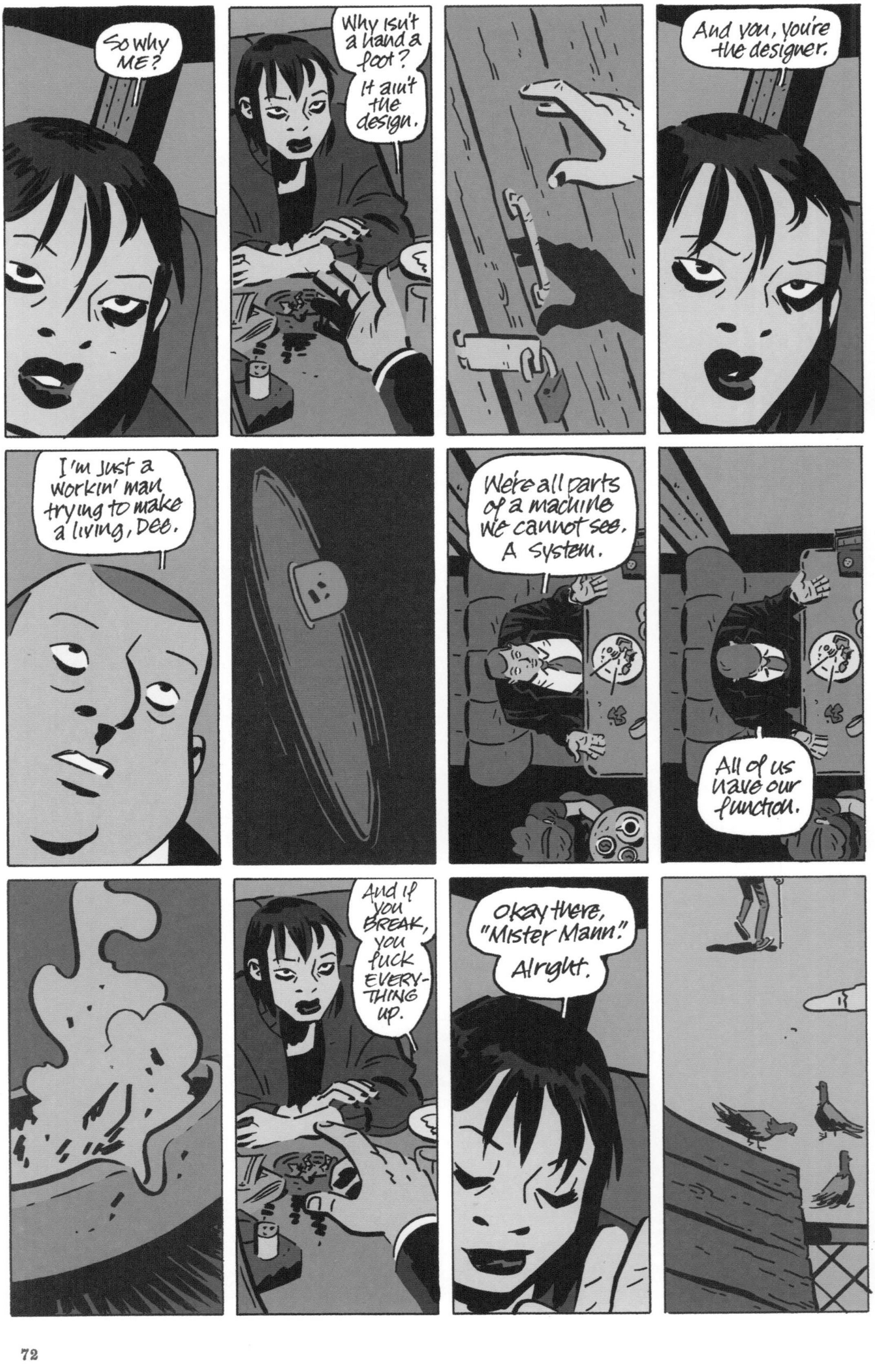
So why ME?
Why isn't a hand a foot? It ain't the design.
And you, you're the designer.
I'm just a workin' man trying to make a living, Dee.
We're all parts of a machine we cannot see. A system.
All of us have our function.
And if you BREAK, you fuck EVERYTHING up.
Okay there, "Mister Mann." Alright.

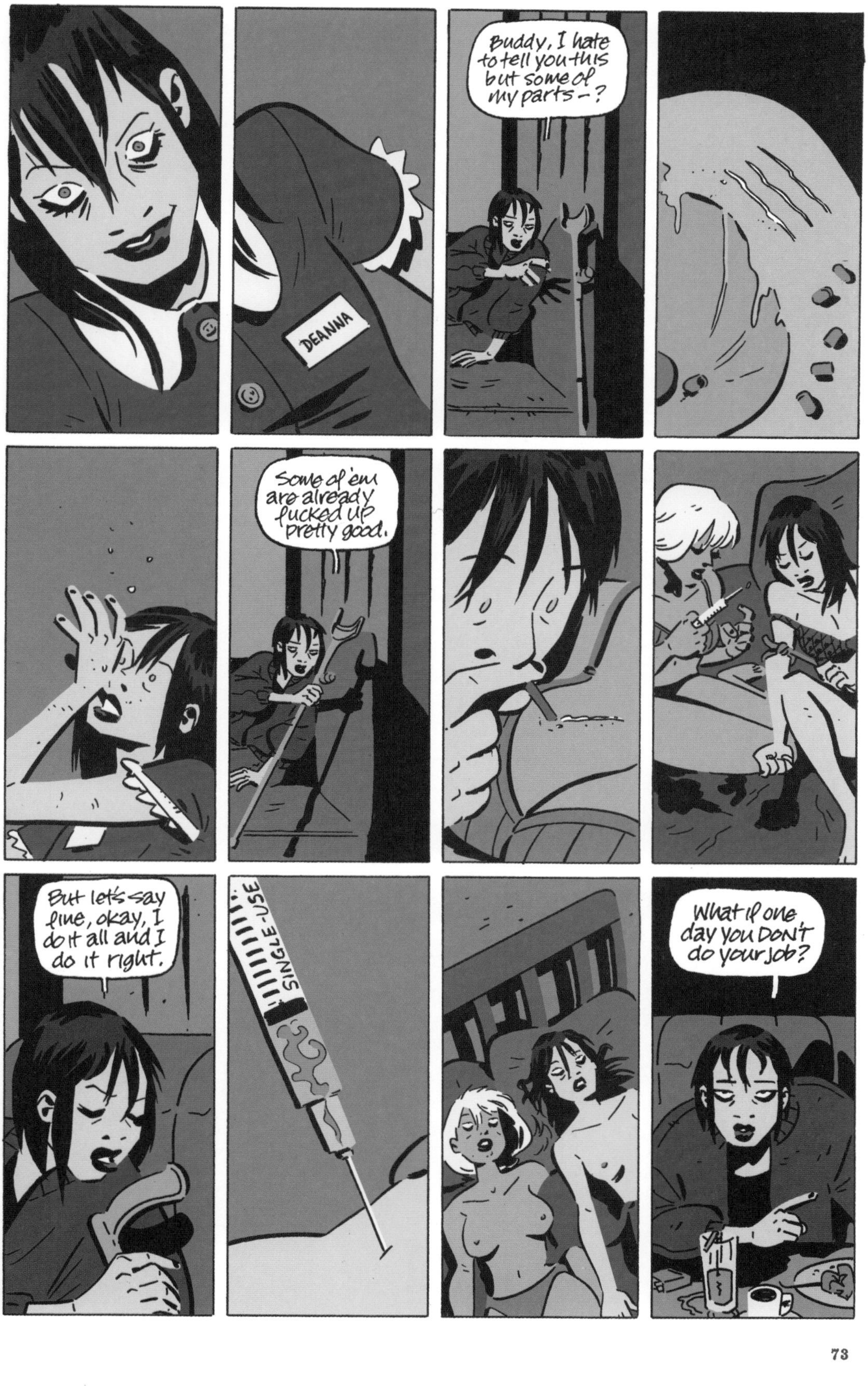
DEANNA
Buddy, I hate to tell you this but some of my parts – ?
Some of 'em are already fucked up pretty good.
But let's say fine, okay, I do it all and I do it right.
SINGLE-USE
What if one day you DON'T do your job?

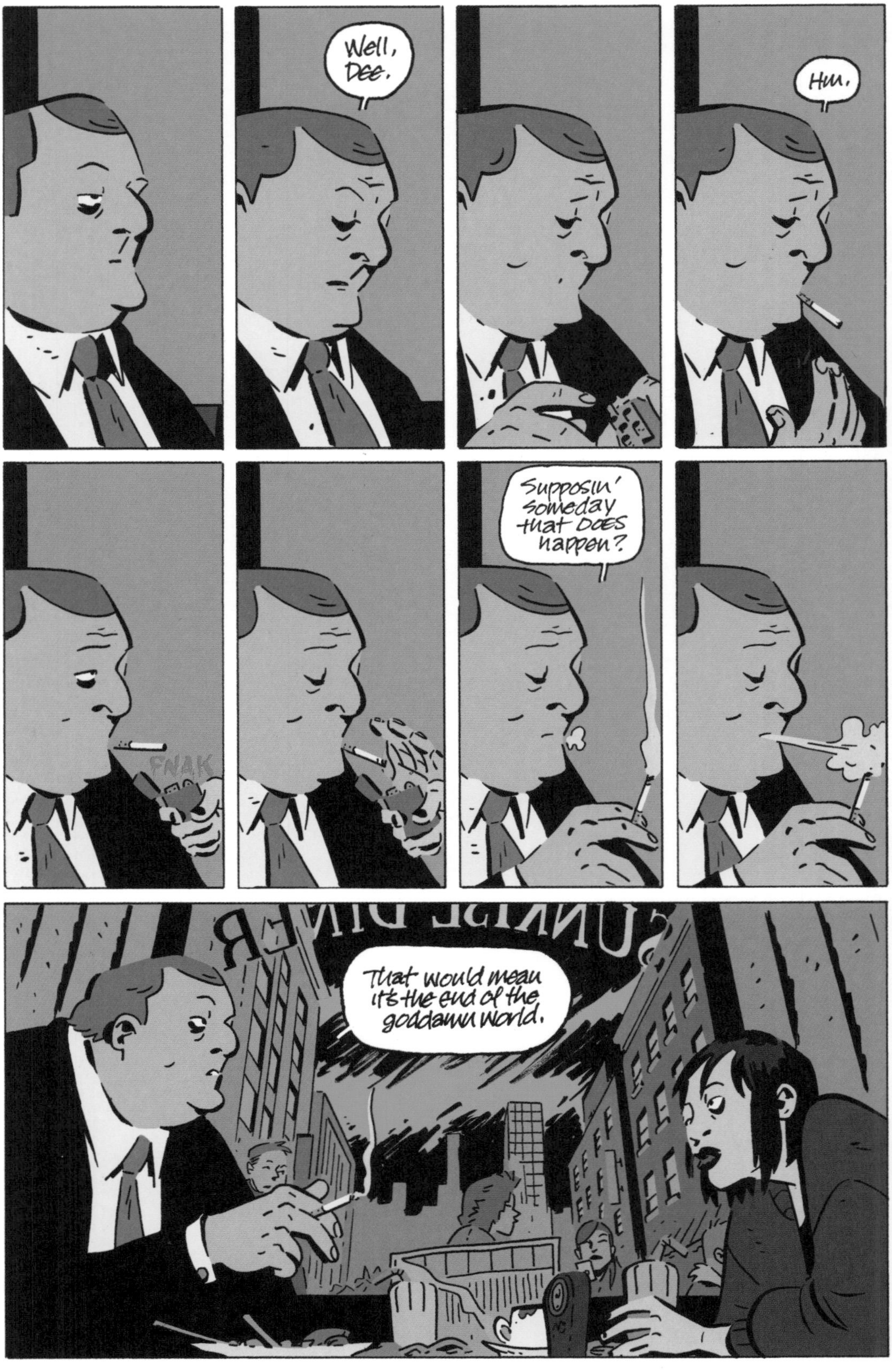
Well, Dee.
Hm.
FNAK
Supposin' someday that DOES happen?
That would mean it's the end of the goddamn world.

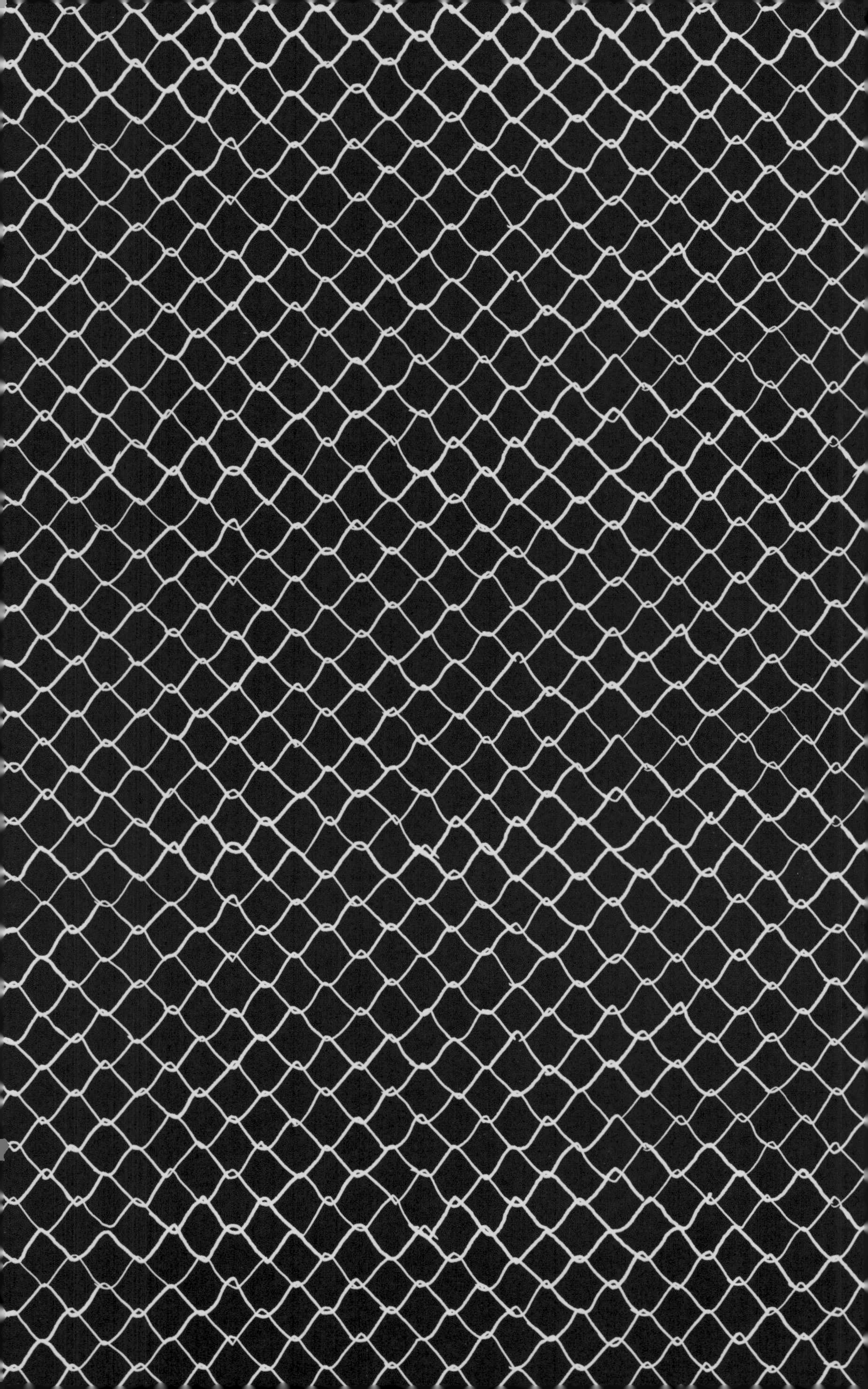

MATT FRACTION
WRITER

ELSA CHARRETIER
ARTIST

MATT HOLLINGSWORTH
COLORIST

KURT ANKENY
LETTERER

RIAN HUGHES
DESIGNER

DEANNA PHELPS
PRODUCTION

LAUREN SANKOVITCH
EDITOR

NOVEMBER CREATED BY
MATT FRACTION AND ELSA CHARRETIER

MATT FRACTION writes comic books out in the woods and lives with his wife, writer Kelly Sue DeConnick, his two children, two dogs, a cat, a bearded dragon, and a yard full of coyotes and crows. Surely there's a metaphor there. He's a New York Times bestselling donkus of comics like SEX CRIMINALS (winner of the 2014 Will Eisner Award for Best New Series and named TIME Magazine's Best Comic of 2013), ODY-C, and CASANOVA. Fraction and DeConnick are currently developing television for Legendary TV under their company Milkfed Criminal Masterminds, Inc.

ELSA CHARRETIER is a writer and comic book artist. After debuting on COWL at Image Comics, Elsa co-created THE INFINITE LOOP with writer Pierrick Colinet at IDW. She has since worked at DC Comics (STARFIRE, BOMBSHELLS, HARLEY QUINN), Marvel Comics (THE UNSTOPPABLE WASP), and Random House (WINDHAVEN, written by George R.R. Martin). She has also written THE INFINITE LOOP vol. 2 as well as SUPERFREAKS, and is a regular artist on STAR WARS comic books.

MATT HOLLINGSWORTH has been coloring comics professionally since 1991 and has worked on titles such as PREACHER, WYTCHES, HAWKEYE, DAREDEVIL, HELLBOY, CATWOMAN, THOR, THE FILTH, WOLVERINE, and PUNISHER, among others. He's currently working on BATMAN: CURSE OF THE WHITE KNIGHT for DC Comics as well as SEVEN TO ETERNITY and NOVEMBER for Image Comics. He's won more awards for the beers he's brewed than for the comics he's colored.

KURT ANKENY is an award-winning cartoonist and painter whose work has appeared in Best American Comics, the Society of Illustrators, the Cape Ann Museum, Comics Workbook, Ink Brick, PEN America's Illustrated PEN, and Fantagraphics's NOW anthology. He lives with his wife and son in Salem, Massachusetts.

RIAN HUGHES is a graphic designer, illustrator, comic artist, writer, and typographer who has written and drawn comics for 2000AD and BATMAN: BLACK AND WHITE, and designed logos for James Bond, the X-Men, Superman, Hed Kandi and The Avengers. His comic strips have been collected in Yesterday's Tomorrows and Tales from Beyond Science, and his burlesque portraits in Soho Dives, Soho Divas. The recent Logo a Gogo collects many of his logo designs for the comic book world and beyond.

IMAGE COMICS, INC.
Robert Kirkman : Chief Operating Officer
Erik Larsen : Chief Financial Officer
Todd McFarlane : President
Marc Silvestri : Chief Executive Officer
Jim Valentino : Vice President
Eric Stephenson : Publisher / Chief Creative Officer
Jeff Boison : Director of Publishing Planning & Book Trade Sales
Chris Ross : Director of Digital Sales
Jeff Stang : Director of Direct Market Sales
Kat Salazar : Director of PR & Marketing
Drew Gill : Art Director
Heather Doornink : Production Director
Nicole Lapalme : Controller
IMAGECOMICS.COM

NOVEMBER, VOL. 1.
First printing.
November 2019.
Published by Image Comics, Inc.
Office of publication : 2701 NW Vaughn St., Suite 780,
Portland, OR 97210.
Copyright © 2019 Milkfed Criminal Masterminds, Inc.
& Big Head Little Arms SAS.
All rights reserved.
For international rights,
Contact : foreignlicensing@imagecomics.com.
ISBN : 978-1-5343-1354-5.

For more information on other Milkfed Criminal Masterminds, Inc.
titles, go to www.milkfed.us/books.

NEXT:
THE GUN IN THE PUDDLE

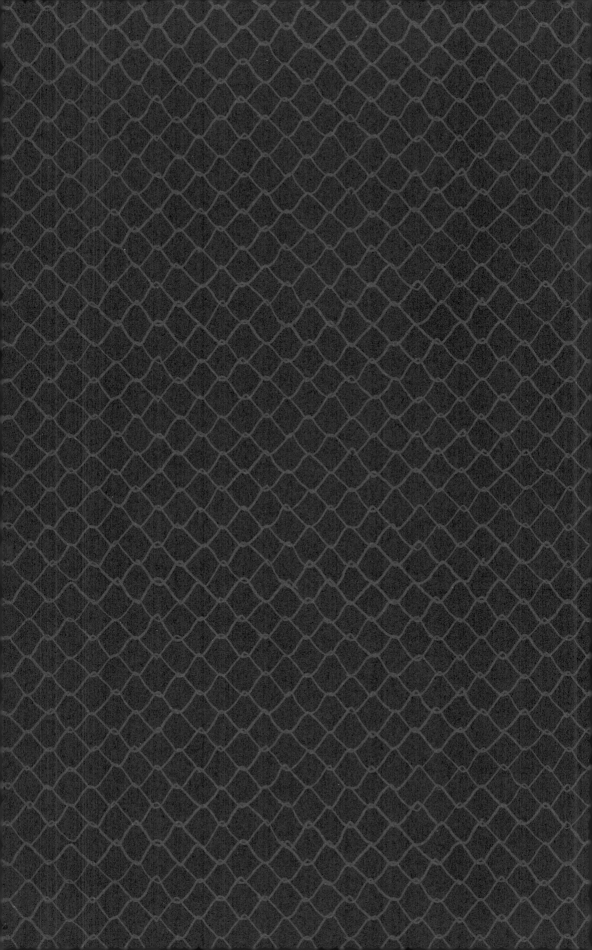